❧ CHILD OF THE AIR ❧

Also by Grace Chetwin

Picture Books
MR. MEREDITH AND THE
TRULY REMARKABLE STONE
BOX AND COX

For Older Readers
COLLIDESCOPE
ON ALL HALLOWS' EVE
OUT OF THE DARK WORLD

Books about Gom Gobblechuck
GOM ON WINDY MOUNTAIN
THE RIDDLE AND THE RUNE
THE CRYSTAL STAIR
THE STARSTONE

GRACE CHETWIN

CHILD
OF
THE
AIR

BRADBURY PRESS / NEW YORK

COLLIER MACMILLAN CANADA / TORONTO
MAXWELL MACMILLAN INTERNATIONAL PUBLISHING GROUP
NEW YORK / OXFORD / SINGAPORE / SYDNEY

Bradbury Press
Macmillan Publishing Company
866 Third Avenue
New York, NY 10022

Collier Macmillan Canada, Inc.
1200 Eglinton Avenue East
Suite 200
Don Mills, Ontario M3C 3N1

FIRST EDITION

Printed and bound in the United States of America
10 9 8 7 6 5 4 3 2 1

The text of this book is set in Garamond No. 3.
Book design by Cathy Bobak

Library of Congress Cataloging-in-Publication Data
Chetwin, Grace.
Child of the air / by Grace Chetwin. — 1st ed.
p.   cm.
Summary: When Grandpa dies Myl and her brother Brevan are made
geth, throwaways who become slaves to the townsfolk, until the
children discover that they can fly.
ISBN 0-02-718317-3
[1. Fantasy. 2. Brothers and sisters—Fiction.] I. Title.
PZ7.C42555Ch   1991
[Fic]—dc20   90-47565

For Ruth & Shirley

PART
FIRST

CHAPTER 1

The two children toiled up the steep hillslope, hauling on the empty broom cart, impatient to get home. Their grandfather, leery of slick clay underfoot, trod more cautiously behind. The issalm—ice season—might well be over, but wet from the thaw still pooled in the doft, making a hazard for old and brittle bones.

Reaching their hut, Mylanfyndra stretched, looking up into clear sky a deeper blue today, with a good hour of gold left in it, just begging to be spent. "We can't go in yet, Brevan," she declared. "It's far too nice."

"Oh, really?" Her brother jabbed the wet doft with his toe. "And just what would we do in this, Myl?"

"What we always do after the issalm," Mylanfyndra said, pointing up behind the hut. "Grandpa! Grandpa!" She ran to meet the broom-maker. "Let's climb to the Grandpa Grove!"

"The Grandpa Grove?" Gven'bahr-brum peered up through the podliths, frowning. "Mylanfyndra, girl, it's too soon. The air still gets cold so fast, don't let this sunlight fool you."

"*Please,* Grandpa?"

"We'll go up in a day or two, when my old legs are back in stride. By then, the air will keep its warmth a little longer."

"We needn't stay," Mylanfyndra persisted. "Just go straight up and down again, promise!"

"I'll say!" Gven retorted. "All our brooms sold and folk clamoring for more now the open doft down there is drying out and filling their houses with dust! We'll be working past bedtime, even so, to keep up with demand."

"Hah!" Brevan snorted, putting in his half-grat's worth. They all knew how the hut was stacked with brooms, fruit of an issalm's laboring!

Gven sighed. "The day is fine, I must admit. Very well, we stay out one more hour—no longer! Go on, go ahead, I'll take my own good time. Careful!" he warned, as they rushed away behind the hut and up through the tangled podlithra. "Watch for barbs—and remember the stip is rising. Don't get any on your clothes!"

They climbed single file, Brevan leading—but not fast enough for Mylanfyndra. "Step lively, will you? We want some time for a game," she complained, and promptly slipped. Not her fault entirely. A round, ungainly bird, head down in urgent quest for vinesuckers and 'lithworms, had waddled out underfoot, and how to see, Mylanfyndra thought irritably, when the drab gray plumage merged so

4

well into the doft? A firebird, wingless now, and a ghost of its plump self after an issalm's fasting! With a loud squawk, it scuttled off among the podliths as Mylanfyndra's feet slid under her. In her fall, she grabbed for a podlith limb, missed, and went down, the limb's barbed tip snagging her sleeve. "Ow!" She came up, hands and knees all clay.

Brevan looked back. "Are you all right, Myl?"

Mylanfyndra checked. Luckily, the barb had missed her skin, but her coat sleeve was torn, and worse, her skirt was smeared with sticky vine sap. In only hours, the stip would harden into stone, and her one good working dress would be ruined. "Just look at that!" she cried in vexation.

"Here, Myl." Brevan pointed to a nearby puddle. "Wash it out, quick."

Crouching, Mylanfyndra swished the sticky patch around in the puddle, rinsing out the milky stip. After squeezing out the excess water, she moved on, wet skirt clinging. Now, despite her haste, she climbed more carefully up to their goal: a round, bald knoll crowned with a ring of hoary podliths, the oldest in the podlithra. Their living vine—leoia—long since gone, the hollow, upright stumps made splendid hiding places. It was for these aged ancestors that the children had named the place the Grandpa Grove.

Mylanfyndra sighed with satisfaction as the jagged pillars came into view. "Koos is gone, the issalm is over!" she cried, and felt secure.

"Maybe," warned Brevan. "But with Koos gone, can Anlahr be far behind?"

"The glair won't be here for two whole seasons—the far

side of the year," Mylanfyndra retorted. "Why do you always have to take the fun out?" Brevan could tell the year's wheel as well as any; name its quarters with their double seasons as shown in tile on the Moot Hall entrance thuswise:

Nettled, Mylanfyndra turned from him to look for Gven. "Grandpa's taking his time," she murmured. She crossed to the biggest and most majestic podlith bole—a fragment standing taller than Gven himself. Reaching on tiptoe, Mylanfyndra peered into the caisson through a massive hole in the side. Not that there was much to see, save tangled root tubes at the base, and space under them where the doft had eroded. She stroked the bole's rough outer surface, still damp from the thaw. Grandpa's favorite podlith. Come warmer weather, he'd sit with his back against this bole, while she and Brevan played their made-up games. Games! Mylanfyndra spun around. Time was wasting. "Let's start a game, quick," she cried.

"Wait." Brevan was stooping low, scanning the ground. "Let's do Pick-a-Shoot first."

"Oh, all right." Frowning, Mylanfyndra joined the search through the tender new leoia shoots poking from the doft like fingertips. Exposed to the air, each tip hardened within hours to form a callus. In a single day, the callus changed to a spiky barb; a tiny, conical hat, with needle point and razor rim. From a row of pores around the rim, the growing vine exuded soft, creamy stip, spiraling it into a tube. In no time, soft tube set into hard, stone casing; both prop and shield to the vine it enclosed. Every first spring visit to the grove, the children each staked out a hopeful shoot and bet on whose would be the bigger by spring's end— eighty or so days hence.

Mylanfyndra pounced. "This one! I pick this one!" she cried, pointing down, just as the broom-maker climbed into view, looking quite puffed.

"Agh, you choose too quickly, Myl," Brevan jeered. "That's why you never win!"

"Now, you two." Gven leaned against the nearest bole. "Hurry, get your visit over. It's turning chill already, didn't I say it would?"

Seemed quite hot to Mylanfyndra. "A minute, Grandpa," she wheedled. "Just one, *please?*"

"Until I get back my wind."

Mylanfyndra turned on Brevan. "A game, quick."

Brevan shrugged. "What game can we play, in no time?"

"Koos and Anlahr." Her favorite. They knew it so well, they could rattle it off. "I'll take Anlahr—and I'll go first, as usual."

Brevan grinned. "You don't say. All right, I'll be Koos, and go second—as usual."

They mounted the knoll, then turned to face each other. Mylanfyndra struck a pose, feet apart, arms raised. "I, Anlahr, winged fire-spirit, do scorch the mesa and set the very air alight with the flames of my breath. I, who bring the glair upon the people am the greatest of all spirits!"

Brevan folded his arms. "Not so, O Anlahr! I, Koos, sharp-heeled ice-giant, do chill your fiery breath and freeze your embers. With issalm do I quell your glair!" He turned away, and started down, but Mylanfyndra caught his sleeve.

"We can't run the podlith ring until we vow to chase each other at opposite ends of the year. It won't make sense."

"I thought we had to rush." Brevan pulled free. "Come on, you're wasting time."

"You're the one who's wasting time," she cried. "Arguing again, as—"

The sound of coughing startled them. The broom-maker, still standing where they'd left him, all bent over.

"Grandpa!" The children ran to him. Gven's face was dark red, the veins on his forehead bulged with the strain of his spasm. Presently, he straightened, wiping his eyes. "I'm fine," he said. "I just need to wet my whistle. Come on," he went on, taking them by the hand, and Mylanfyndra felt his shiver. "We have much work to do tonight."

After supper, Mylanfyndra mended her coat sleeve, while

Brevan sorted broomstraw, the fine droppings of dead vine ends, into brush-sized bales. Gven, his long legs stretched to the fire, set to for a while knotting fresh vine into fancy broom handles for the richer houses. But despite Gven's threats of working past bedtime, they actually retired early.

Mylanfyndra peered through the dying firelight at the huddled shape in the opposite corner. Gven seemed very tired tonight. She stretched gingerly, wriggling her toes down into the cold sheets. Come to think, so was she, after all the fresh air and climbing. And Brevan, no less, in his neighboring cot along the wall. Asleep already, by the sound of it. She turned about to face him, eyeing the shape of his back. What a fine day it had been. All their brooms sold out! Those townsfolk in their houses, where would they be without Gven to help keep their houses clean! So proud, she'd felt, at the welcome the broom-maker had received. It had been good to visit the town again—and just as good to leave it!

Those town children, thought Mylanfyndra, her eyes closing, in their grand houses with huge larders, and closets full of clothes, and roofs higher than Gven on tiptoe—she wouldn't want to live down there for all the half-grats on the mesa!

Embers shifted in the hearth, flame flared for an instant, throwing strong shadows onto the layered walls: walls built of long, thin 'lith shards stacked horizontally. Then it subsided, spent, and all was still and quiet.

"Myl! Myl—wake up!"

Mylanfyndra opened her eyes. For a moment, she stared

unfocussed at bare hut wall. Then she became aware that Brevan's cot was empty, the covers thrown back. She turned to face the room.

"Brevan?" In his nightshirt, holding up a lantern.

"Get up, Myl." He looked frightened.

She scrambled off the cot, her blanket falling away. The warmth from the fire was long since gone; the chill air reeked of ashes. Mylanfyndra shuddered as the cold struck through. "What is it, what's wrong?"

Before Brevan could answer, an eerie sound started from the opposite corner of the hut. Low, and quiet, and faintly rasping, it swelled to a groan, as if someone squeezed a ghastly bellows. Mylanfyndra peered wide-eyed toward the far wall. *"Grandpa?"*

Brevan nodded, following her gaze.

Mylanfyndra sped barefoot across the cold clay tile. Gven's eyes were shut, and his face looked drained. "Grandpa?" She touched his shoulder lightly. *"Grandpa!"*

A spasm seized Gven's chest. Mylanfyndra snatched back her hand, remembering his earlier one up on the knoll. The gray flesh suffused with blood, the veins on his forehead stood out as his body jerked with the force of his coughing. "I think he's really sick," she said uneasily.

"Sick?" Brevan looked at her in disbelief.

Gven'bahr-brum was never sick. Not in the issalm, when folk took to bed in droves with ice-fever; not during the glair, when they dropped in the Warren's tunnel shelters like zyt-flies from the deadly heat and humidity. "Grandpa's the fittest person on all the mesa," Brevan said loudly.

Mylanfyndra stood firm. "Maybe," she said, "but he doesn't sound that way right now."

CHAPTER 2

 "What do we do, Brevan?" Mylanfyn-
dra looked into his eyes, and saw her own concern reflected
there. But Brevan only shrugged.

"We wait."

"How long?"

"Until he wakes." Brevan retreated to the hearth.

"And then?" Mylanfyndra followed.

"I don't know." Setting down the lamp, Brevan reached
for kindling, and piled it in the faint warmth of last night's
embers. "Come on," he urged, as the old man gave voice
to another bout, "help me light this fire."

Mylanfyndra lit a taper from the lamp, then set the taper
to the kindling. But she wouldn't touch the bellows. So
Brevan fanned the flames, throwing golden light and drafty
shadows on the layered walls. Mylanfyndra stared into the
bright, new fire. Gven . . . sick! Fear stirred inside her.

For all of her eleven years, or as much as she could recall, life had run its circle. The pattern never varied, so the thought that it might had never occurred.

But now?

Mylanfyndra glanced toward Gven's corner uncertainly. Just then, his cot creaked, starting her up. "Brev? Myl?" His voice was so cracked and dry Mylanfyndra scarcely knew it.

She ran with Brevan to his side.

"Grandpa." Mylanfyndra tried for normal, but the word came out too high and her face felt tight with worry.

"I . . ."—Gven licked the corner of his mouth—"need water. . . ."

They raced for the drinking crock. Brevan got there first. He filled a cup, handed it to Mylanfyndra. She carried it to the old man and put it to his lips. Anxiously, they watched him sip. In the light, his tousled hair was finely haloed. Mylanfyndra gazed down, noting now the jutting nose and cheekbones, the puffy folds beneath the eyes, the silver stubble. Why, he's *old!* she thought, and looked to Brevan, but her brother seemed intent only upon Gven's drinking.

After half a dozen sips, Grandpa pulled away from the cup. "Thank you." He lay back weakly, looking from one to the other, catching their concern. "I've a small chill," he said. "Not to worry. Be gone in a day or two."

Chill. Mylanfyndra gazed down in consternation. Her fault, forcing Gven up to the knoll. Hadn't he warned it was too soon? She recalled his weariness, his shivering. "I'll fetch the apothecary, Grandpa." That's what townsfolk did when sickness struck their house.

"No!" The old man's head snapped up. "Don't even think of it!"

"But he'll give you—"

"I said *no!*" Gven's eyes went wide, the cords stood out in his neck. "And when I say no, I mean—" His voice cracked. He took the cup, closed his hands about it, and took a long drink. Then he handed it back, wiping his hand across his mouth. "Girl: I don't want Ryke. Sleep is all I need."

Mylanfyndra stared. He had never been so fierce, not with her. "I was only trying to help, Grandpa." Brevan must have been puzzled, too, because he said, "Grandpa, if it's the cost—"

"Not cost, not cost!" He shoved the cup at her. "Listen, both of you: don't go into town today. Don't go into the podlithra—in fact, don't go out that door!" Red spots touched Gven's cheeks, then spread all over, and his breathing began to quicken. Abruptly, he reached for Mylanfyndra's hand, closed his own knuckly one around it. "You know I don't want intruders poking around up here."

Mylanfyndra shook her head, still shaken at his outburst. "Only the apothecary, Grandpa."

"Tshhh." He waved them off. "Go make your morning mash, none for me. Go, both of you; go—and do as I tell you." Gven's voice sank to a whisper. He let fall his hand and closed his eyes.

Brevan led her back to the fire.

"Why won't he let me fetch Ryke, Brevan?"

"You heard him. He likes his privacy."

"But if he's really sick—"

"I'm sure he'll change his mind. Look, it's getting light. Let's do as he says and make our mash."

All morning, Mylanfyndra worked with Brevan on the brooms, taking it in turns to bathe the old man's face. Toward noon, he stirred, mumbled something they could not catch, but he did not awaken.

Mylanfyndra cast about for something cheerful to say. "It was so nice up on the knoll yesterday," she began, then faltered, remembering how they never should have gone up there.

"We didn't do much," Brevan said.

"We picked a shoot, and played Koos and Anlahr."

"We never got to finish it."

Or even start it right, thought Mylanfyndra, but kept that to herself. Was there nothing she could safely say? "We'll do it over soon as Grandpa's well. It's still my favorite story, I think. What about you, Brevan?"

Brevan grunted.

"Well, it was last time Grandpa told it—only a few months since," Mylanfyndra went on doggedly. "Imagine," she said, looking up from her work. "Imagine striding the sky as easily as we run around down here! Would you rather be Koos, or Anlahr?"

"Neither," Brevan said flatly. "I like the ground, thank you."

Mylanfyndra made a face. "Don't be such a squadge. You remember when we stayed up all night once, just before the first snows, hoping for a peek at Koos?"

"That was a long time ago," Brevan said. "I believed anything then. They're not real, Myl."

"Not—" Mylanfyndra set down her straw. "You mean to say—you don't believe in them anymore? Brevan!"

He kept his head down. "I can't help how I feel, Myl."

Mylanfyndra set her work deliberately aside. "Gven saw Anlahr pass over this very hut. He saw the bolts of lightning shoot from the heels. Where the bolt struck, the leoia flashed into ash, and the podlith stone shattered, and all around the shards turned black."

Brevan looked up. "Think, Myl. How could Grandpa have seen all this? He's not here during the glair. He's down in the Warren with everyone else."

"Brevan! He was late getting down that year. Lucky he made it at all."

"So he says."

"Brevan!"

"It was long ago, before we were born."

A strange restlessness stirred in Mylanfyndra's chest, quickly swelled to suffocation. "Are you—are you calling Grandpa a liar?"

Brevan looked defiant. "He could have been mistaken. He may have seen a bird, a cutwing, say. They can get pretty big."

"Right before the glair? With all the birds long gone to shelter?"

"A firebird, then. We've spotted them at the very last moment."

"A firebird? With a human body? And lightning streaking from its heels? And long hair streaming out behind?"

Mylanfyndra remembered every word of Grandpa's story, saw the scene as clearly as if she'd been there, too.

Brevan snorted in disbelief. "Myl! Tell me just how would a fire-spirit have hair?"

"It wouldn't be ordinary hair," she countered, but Brevan didn't answer.

Mylanfyndra bent to her work, put out at her brother's revelation. How could he stop believing! Without Koos and Anlahr, how else to explain the months of ice and fire? Why, the whole town believed in them. The townsfolk had even mounted two larger-than-life likenesses above the Moot Hall entrance. On a huge, circular medallion worked in

painted tile, the pair were featured back-to-back, Anlahr worked in gold; Koos, in silver. Stark against a ground of deep blue clay, their craggy profiles gazed out in opposite directions, each seeking the other. In their upraised hands were spears of ice and tongues of fire, poised for throwing. The townsfolk would never have gone to such trouble—

and expense—had the spirits not been real! Anyway, thought Mylanfyndra, Grandpa's word was good enough for her.

"What's gotten into you?" Mylanfyndra eyed her brother resentfully. "Why do you always have to spoil things?" She bent, stiff-lipped, to her work. Let him think what he pleased. He would not diminish her faith in the tales, or her pleasure in their telling.

For a long while after, they didn't speak. Nothing broke the silence save the shift of brands in the hearth, and Gven's troubled breathing. The sun rose over the trees, cast one quick noontide beam across the table. Then the gloom of afternoon set in. Gven awoke once, briefly. The children fetched him water and bathed his face. He told them to heat themselves some broth. But just past sunset, he stirred and called out, seeming not to know them. Then he began to shout and thresh about.

The children hovered, alarmed.

"What's he saying, Brevan?"

"I don't know." Her brother put a finger to his lips.

Mylanfyndra caught Ryke'ven-apoth's name. "Brevan, did you hear?"

"Shush."

Gven's eyes opened wide, staring sightlessly. "No . . . o . . . o . . . o!" The word started low, then slid up to a wail. "No! No! No! Not Ryke! Not Toova'ven-tuil! They mustn't . . . she mustn't find . . ."

Mylanfyndra frowned. *Toova'ven-tuil?*

"What's he saying, Brevan? What does he mean?" Why did Gven speak of the Tollwife?

"Shush." Brevan laid a hand on her arm. "Myl, he's lost his senses."

"Oh, Brevan! I'm fetching Ryke."

"No! He told us not!"

"That was this morning. He doesn't even know us now. If we leave him much longer, he might even die!" The very thought terrified Mylanfyndra. She ran for her coat.

"Myl! What are you doing!"

"What do you think!" she cried, and fled into the night.

CHAPTER 3

Town was not so far, Mylanfyndra told herself. By day, it took less than half an hour to manhandle the broom cart down through the podlithra and out onto open, level ground. Small comfort that was now! Oh, why had she not stopped to take up a lantern—and a shawl: it was freezing! Slipping, sliding, tumbling, she struggled on down sodden slope and bank, Gven's ravings echoing in her ears, until at last the incline leveled out and Mylanfyndra burst through onto open ground. Now at last she could run, over wiregrass and stone, until she reached the first houses. Putting on a spurt, she sped through quiet stone streets, to the apothecary's front gate.

Ryke's windows were dark. Had he gone to bed? Townsfolk retired early, for once the sun went down there was little to do. If he were in bed, she'd be rousting him out.

How would he take that? she wondered, nervously. The neighboring homes were dark, also. Her knocking would sound loud in the quiet. It might wake others, and create a fuss, and that would upset Grandpa even more when he got to hear. As she wavered, rusty iron creaked above her head. Ryke's apothecary sign, swinging in the night wind: a pestle and mortar that during the day flashed rich gold on a deep blue ground. Now the gilded shapes gleamed mystical, hovering in the air. Mylanfyndra gazed up thoughtfully. According to Grandpa, those symbols told the right of any to call out apothecary, day or night. Encouraged, she trod the path, climbed the step, and rapped smartly on the door.

Silence.

Mylanfyndra waited, her courage draining. Had Ryke not heard? Was he perhaps out on another call? She took a deep breath and rapped again. This time, light flared in an upstairs window then vanished. She hopped from one foot to the other, folded her arms about her body: the warmth from running had gone, and she was growing chill.

Steps approached the door. "Who is it?" A pleasant voice, but guarded.

"Gven'bahr-brum's grandchild," Mylanfyndra answered, speaking into the crack 'twixt door and frame.

"What do you want?"

"Grandpa's taken a chill."

"Gven'bahr-brum, you say?" A pause. "He lives up in the podlithra."

"Yes, but you—"

"Oh, I can't go up there in the dark. Come back tomorrow."

"But that might be too late!"

"Oh? Who said that? Your grandfather?"

"Not . . . exactly." Mylanfyndra's teeth began to chatter.

"Then who sent you?"

"I—came on my own."

"On your own? Oh, dear child! Go home!" Ryke called, his voice receding.

Go home? Mylanfyndra stared, dumbstruck. She glanced back to the swinging sign, then, turning once more to the door, she pounded on it with new determination. "This sign says you have to visit the sick!" she yelled. "So come—please: I'll guide you."

Lights sprang in nearby windows. Doors opened. Folk emerged, shining lanterns into the dark. Mylanfyndra watched, dismayed. Worse and worse!

"What's all the racket?" a man demanded. "What's going on?"

"I'm fetching out the apothecary," she answered defiantly.

"Oh?" A woman stepped outside for a closer view. "Who's sick, then?"

Mylanfyndra turned away, pretending not to hear, not wanting to tell.

"Where are you, Ryke?" the woman cried.

"Hey, Ryke, hurry so we can go back to bed!" another neighbor yelled.

The woman shuffled across and swung a lantern over Ryke's fence. "Hey, I know you," she said. "You're Gven'bahr-brum's lass, aren't you?"

Mylanfyndra turned to face her. "Yes."

"Out on this cold night? Oh—what a sight! Your dress is all torn up. And your feet are clogged in doft! And your face!" The woman peered closer. "You've been bled. Is that why you're here?"

"No." The word was out before she could stop it.

"What, then? Is it the old man?"

Mylanfyndra looked the other way.

"What's up, then?" the man called. "Must be bad, to send you out at this hour and in this weather."

To Mylanfyndra's relief, the door opened and Ryke stood wide in hat and cloak, holding his apothecary's bag in one hand, a lighted lantern in the other. "Good people, go in out of the cold or I'll be tending you come morning. If I am not back by dawn, know that I have ventured into the podlithra to tend Gven'bahr-brum." He swung his bag around for all to see. "Here, girl, take this," he said, shoving the lantern into Mylanfyndra's hand, and strode off down the path into the street. Conscious of the watching eyes, Mylanfyndra struggled to keep pace, holding out the lamp.

The man pressed on, saying nothing until they were out of earshot. Then he stopped and rounded on her. "Well," he said, "you got your way, miss. But I warn you: this had better not be some wild chase." He moved closer. "Hold that light more this way, I can't see where I'm going. How do you suppose I'll get through that mess in the dark, eh? By the time I arrive—*if* I arrive—I'll likely be in greater need of remedy than your grandpa. And if so, that will cost," he said, and laughed.

Mylanfyndra held her tongue. A strange man. Tricky, behind the public face. He'd meant that threat, she was sure, yet all the time his voice had stayed so pleasant. She thought of the homeward climb in this man's company— and prayed that he might by some miracle reach the hut unscathed!

The trek was long and exceeding cold, for Ryke crawled at a 'lithworm's pace once they reached the podlithra. Mylanfyndra's hands went numb, the faint warmth from the lantern no match for the bite in the air. To make matters worse, the apothecary grumbled every step of the way—

then even threatened to turn back. But just as Mylanfyndra began to fear Ryke would make good that threat, a small, bright glow appeared: the lighted hut window. As they crossed the clearing, the door flew wide and Brevan ran to meet them.

"Myl! I thought you were hurt!" Reaching her side, he stopped short. "You *are* hurt! Oh, Myl, your face!"

Mylanfyndra put a hand to her cheek. "It's just a scratch."

"But why didn't you have it tended?" Brevan looked pointedly at the apothecary, but the man walked past as if Brevan weren't there, up the step and through the door. They hurried after him.

The man was just inside, gazing around with wrinkled nose, just as though, thought Mylanfyndra, the place smelled bad. Come to think—she sniffed in mingled scents of smoke, and soot, and broomstraw, and the stale, sour must of old man—it was a little close inside. But it was a good, familiar smell: homely, and reassuring, especially to one coming in from a cold spring night.

Ryke took off his cloak, revealing wide, bent shoulders, barrel chest and round, pot belly. "Here, boy. Put this somewhere . . . clean," he said, and moved to Gven's cot. Mylanfyndra edged near for a glimpse of her grandfather, but the apothecary waved her back. He felt Gven's brow, then put his ear to the old man's chest. Presently, he straightened, and looked around. "Lad, clear the table. I need space." He turned to Mylanfyndra. "And you: get hot water and a clean—I said *clean*—dry pot."

They scurried to obey. Brevan scooped the clutter off the tabletop and stashed it underneath while Mylanfyndra filled the kettle from the crock and set it on the hearthplate. Then she took the battered mash pot, and scrubbed off lingering specks of the morning's meal. Clean, indeed! What right had Ryke to speak to them like that? And to imply that they lived dirty? She slapped the pot down onto the newly cleared space as smartly as she dared.

The apothecary set his bag on the table, and waved them off. "Away now. Children have no place in sickrooms. Out, and let me get on with my work."

They stood their ground.

"There's nowhere to go," Mylanfyndra said.

"Only here," Brevan chipped in.

Ryke pointed to the door. "There's out there—if you get in my way."

Fuming, they went to sit crosslegged on their cots, while the man fished out small packets of red, and blue, and yellow, and white powders from his bag, and shook a few grains from each into the mash pot. Squashing his belly into the table, he stirred them in together by means of a long glass rod.

Mylanfyndra craned her neck, wishing she could see; all those separate powders—what was each for? And what did they look like, what did they make now, all mingled in together? She started to ask, but Brevan signaled her to hush. Yet the questions kept coming. As each popped up, she pushed it off, mindful of Ryke's threat. But at last, despite her struggles, her most pressing worry broke through. "Will he soon be better?"

"Hush, Myl," Brevan warned, but Ryke did not even look up. Did that mean Gven might not soon get well? Mylanfyndra thought anxiously. Or . . . not at all! "How—how bad is Grandpa?" she ventured.

"How bad?" The apothecary's head came up now. "I'd say he's worse than well, yet better than dead." He bent once more to his task, his back curving like a length of vine. "If you must help, dip some cloth in that tub outside. He needs his head cooled down."

Released from confinement, they raced to obey. Mylanfyndra dipped her rag into the water, shuddered at the shock of cold. "Come on," she said, her teeth clicking. "Let's get back in."

"Just a minute, Myl." Brevan tore a strip off his rag, dunked it, squeezed it out, then dabbed her cheek. "It's nasty," he said, peering at the wound. "Ryke should put salve on it."

"Oh, come on, Brevan." Mylanfyndra pushed up a sleeve, revealing an arm crisscrossed with scars and abrasions. "It's no worse than these. I'll be fine," she protested, pleased at Brevan's concern, even so.

They folded up their icy rags and took them inside. Ryke, his back turned, crouched before the hearth, stirring the mash pot over the flames. They crept across into Gven's corner.

"His chest is hardly moving," Brevan whispered. "He is breathing?"

Mylanfyndra leaned down. If she put her ear really close, she could still detect air squeezing through the old man's windpipe. "I think he's just quieted down." She placed her wet pack carefully on Gven's brow, while Brevan laid his at the crown. They lingered, hoping for some flicker from

Grandpa's face, until Ryke chased them back to their cots. The apothecary slipped dark liquid down Gven's throat. Then he produced a small jar of bright green paste that filled the hut with stinging vapor. Ryke daubed some on his hands, and rubbed the old man's flat, bony chest. Then, wiping his hands down his coat, he dropped jar and packets back inside his bag. "You, laddie," Ryke crooked a finger, "you walk me down. After . . ." He extended his palm.

The man's fee! Mylanfyndra hadn't thought! She turned to Brevan, dismayed—to find him calmly holding out a half-grat coin. She stared. How had he gotten that?

Ryke was shaking his head. "Fee's double for night calls."

To Mylanfyndra's further amazement, Brevan fished in a pocket and drew out a second coin, placed them both on Ryke's outstretched hand.

"Umph." Ryke's eyes narrowed. "For one moment I thought we had a situation here." He turned to the door. "Well, put on your coat and let's be gone, if I'm to get some sleep this night."

"What about Grandpa?" Mylanfyndra demanded, as Brevan took up the lamp.

"Leave him be. Get to bed. Someone will be by at sunup."

"But—" Mylanfyndra ran after him. "Grandpa said he doesn't want—"

"He's not going to quarrel. The door please."

What did Ryke mean, not going to quarrel? His smile now seemed full of menace. "Grandpa said it was a chill, just a chill," she argued, opening the door. Biting wind cut in, riffling her thin sleeves, spiking her flesh.

Ryke stepped past without a glance, nudging Brevan out

before him, and strode away to the edge of the clearing. "Hold that lantern higher, laddie. If I come to grief—so do you," Mylanfyndra heard him say, then his voice faded into the dark.

She watched the light spark in and out the stony thickets, farther and farther away until it vanished. For a moment, Mylanfyndra stood, numb with the awfulness of everything, until, realizing how cold it was, she closed the door. Grandpa looked better—or was it just the glow from the fire?

"Grandpa?" she said quietly, leaning over. "Grandpa, can you hear me?"

No answer.

"Sorry about Ryke, but I had to bring him." She straightened up. When he awoke, he would be most put out with her, and with Brevan, no less, she thought, remembering how Brevan had paid Ryke's fee—with coins from Grandpa's locker! Such boldness!

Mylanfyndra huddled down beside the cot to await Brevan's return. Poor Brevan, she pitied him his journey. A dangerous man, Ryke. If others were like him beneath their friendly smiles and greetings, small wonder now why Grandpa kept those folk at arm's length! She sighed. What a mess. To think that only hours before the worst she had on her mind was a torn coat sleeve and stip down her skirt! She gazed critically around the hut. Looked smaller, now Ryke had gone. The man had filled the place, leaving no room for maneuver. She stared at the bare tabletop, remembering the bulbous body bent over it. Ryke would be back on the morrow—with goodness knew who else!

She clapped her hands to the sides of her head. Gven was getting sicker, that was what Ryke had meant. When her brother came back, they must decide how to hold folk at bay. Whatever they had started, they must find a way to stop it, somehow!

CHAPTER 4

The latch clicked, Brevan tumbled in.
"They're coming! First thing!"

Mylanfyndra leapt from her cot. "Who? Who's coming?"

Brevan crossed to the hearth and knelt, rubbing his hands
and spreading them to the warmth. She crouched beside
him. "Who, Brevan? Who're 'they'?"

"A whole crowd of folk. Myl, why would they want to
come up here? And what's the rush?"

"I don't know." Mylanfyndra thought uneasily of Gven's
broken mumblings. "Was Toova with them? Oh, Brevan!"
she cried at his nod. "Why? Why would she come up here,
just because Gven has taken ill?"

"It's her job to know what's going on, I suppose."

"But only if there's a toll to be paid." No one gave birth,
or wed, or took sick, or died without the town exacting
levy. And it was Toova's job to collect that levy, to the last

half-grat. The times Mylanfyndra passed the Tollwife on the street, the woman's sharp glance left her feeling uneasy, even threatened. Other folk didn't bother her, in fact, she'd like to have made friends with some, even if she never said so. But Toova's presence scared her. "The levy isn't on the sick, Brevan. It's on the apothecary's fee, which she could collect down there."

"True." Brevan sat back on his heels. "Look, Myl, maybe we're getting stewed up about nothing. I mean, Gven won't like it when he finds folk up here, and we'll be sure to get a scolding. But there's no threat in it."

"How do we know?" Mylanfyndra eyed her brother doubtfully. "The way Gven said her name; I can't get it out of my mind."

"He said Ryke's, too, Myl."

"I know. But . . . Toova scares me. She knows everybody's business."

"So? What's to know about us? Anyway, as I said, it's just her job."

"It's a rotten job, and she can't be nice to be doing it."

Brevan shrugged. "The Elders set the tolls and Toova gets them paid; how else would they maintain the town? The mesa's so high, the water's so deep it takes two pumpmen to keep the public wells filled. Without tolls, how else would the men be paid?"

Mylanfyndra scowled. "Now you talk of wells! I'm still scared about those people coming up, Brevan. And especially Toova."

Brevan threw his hands into the air. "Why do you keep on? I'm scared, too, but I ask you: what can we do about it? How's Grandpa, anyway?"

"Better, I think, come look."

The old man lay on his back, slack-jawed, eyes shut. His chest under the covers seemed scarce to rise at all. "He seems the same to me, Myl."

"Ryke's remedies are working," Mylanfyndra said firmly. "You'll see."

"Maybe." Brevan turned away. "Is there any broth? I'm starving."

They sat by the hearth, cupping their brew, staring into the fire. "I can't believe this day, can you?" said Mylanfyndra.

Her brother shook his head, avoiding her eye. In that moment, Mylanfyndra knew his thought for it was hers, and a new fear crept in.

During the last glair, while they sheltered in the Warren: the gong booming through the caverns. A man rousting them from their cave. "Come, Gven'bahr-brum. It is between storms. There's to be a Sending."

"Agh, I shall not come. I have no truck with such."

"But you shall," the man insisted. "All take part; it is town custom."

"I am not of the town."

"While you shelter here, you are. Come, bear witness; the children too."

"What's a Sending, Grandpa?" Brevan asked, when the man had gone.

"Some have died," Gven replied gruffly. "So now the dead are sent."

"Sent? Where?"

"Agh! I wish I knew!" Gven pulled on his boots, looking strangely put out. "I would have spared you this, but you see I have no choice."

"Oh." Mylanfyndra was secretly glad of something new, as was Brevan. Eagerly, the children trod the drafty tunnels with Gven to the main assembly hall, where the whole town was gathered, looked like. Mylanfyndra stretched on tiptoe, craning to see. "Where's the dead one?"

"Shush," Gven said.

Mylanfyndra waited, wondering what would happen next. Suddenly, a gong crashed, making her cry out. At the signal, everybody turned toward the cavern's center. A hush, while Mylanfyndra's heart calmed down. Then, all at once, voices shattered the silence, starting her up again.

"Aaaaah! Aaaaaah! Marn is gone! Gone! Gone! What shall we do? How shall we live without our father!"

"Aieeeee! Aieeeee!" A woman's raw wail. "Udrigan! Udrigan—gone also! Who can deny it? Me—I'd give my life to bring my husband back!"

Everybody gradually joined in, the shouting grew wilder and wilder. Mylanfyndra shrank into Gven's side, afraid. These townsfolk, so quiet and civilized: they now seemed quite demented, even violent. She shut her eyes and covered her ears. Is this what they always did when someone died? Brevan tugged her arm. "Look, Myl."

At the center of the cavern, three bodies cased in cloth were raised above the crowd—one of them just the children's size. Mylanfyndra realized that no one had cried the child's name; no one had bewailed its passing. But no time to ask why for now the crowd was making for the cavern entrance.

"We're going *outside,* Grandpa?"

Gven leaned down. "They're sending those bodies off the mesa."

"You mean—off the *cliff?*"

"Aye."

"But *why?*"

"To join the wyrth," Gven said. "Now don't be afraid."

The wyrth? Mylanfyndra felt a thrill of excitement. The wyrth! The spirits who dwelt below the cliffs, wrapping the mesa in mystery. Spirits, who, with the mist—their very substance—screened their secret regions from the mesa folk above. Sometimes, in the mellow season after the glair, the mist crawled onto the mesa, and through the streets, smothering the huddled, stone houses. It seeped through cracks and curled down chimneys, filling every corner with a strange, sick smell. On those days, folk stayed indoors and kept their windows shut against dangerous influences— (ordinary folk, they said, meddled with stuff of spirits on pain of death); and they lit candles and set out pots of dried stoneflowers to mask the smell. But whatever the season, the wyrth never left the cliff edge, never parted to reveal what lay below or beyond the cliff top.

Mylanfyndra had never seen the wyrthwall close to, for Gven had never taken them to the mesa's edge. She and Brevan had only glimpsed the top of it from afar; thin mistcloud fading into the sky. Now here they were, on their way to stand before it. Not only that, now she'd get to see how things looked above ground during the glair!

Mylanfyndra stared into the fire, remembering quite

clearly the shock of blinding light, the molten sky, the hot, dry prickle of her skin. . . .

And there! The wyrthwall, higher than a house; a moving veil of impenetrable white surging into the copper sky. She gazed into the wyrth, trying vainly to pierce it, wondering how thick it was, and how far down it went. Gven didn't know; not even he had tried to find out.

Silent now, the crowd edged cautiously along the clay strip between cavern mouth and cliff, Gven and the children with them. Suddenly, the flash of metal caught Mylanfyndra's eye. "What's that, Grandpa?" A curious structure at the brink; a sort of scaffold: high steps climbing above their heads to a polished slide that curved way out into the mist.

"They call it the Chute." Gven seemed to grow tighter by the minute.

"What's it for?" Brevan said.

"Watch," he said shortly.

The crowd parted, and the bearers carried the bodies slowly up the steps to the top of the Chute. Then, one by one, they let the bodies go. The shrouded figures slid down, gathering speed, and shot into space. For a moment, each hovered light as an ash-feather against the burning sky. Then, slowly, it arced down, and was swallowed by the wyrth.

Folk turned to go back inside, but some climbed the steps and dropped gifts down the Chute: for the wyrth, Gven said. Coins, vials of perfume and oil, and sweetmeats. Tributes to buy good welcome for the newly dead.

The wryth also took their toll.

Now the Sending was done, and the dead were out of sight, Gven seemed to relax. Still he would not let them linger to watch the last tributes go down the Chute. Mylanfyndra was puzzled. She had rarely seen Gven so upset. Was it over the way the dead were sent? Or the thought of death itself? As they reached their little cave, she resolved to find out.

"Why do you not like Sendings, Grandpa?" she began.

"Never mind." He still sounded put out. "We'll not discuss such now, all right?"

"But why not?" Brevan demanded. "There's no harm."

Gven's voice rose. "Who mentioned harm, boy? It's no fit subject for children."

"But one of those sent was a child," Mylanfyndra cut in. "Is it—"

"Enough!" Gven cried. Relenting, he went on quietly, "When you're older, we may speak of death again. But not now—and that's my final word."

Mylanfyndra scrambled to her feet. "Gven is fine. In fact, he's a whole lot better already, as I said."

"But—what about tomorrow?"

"Those people, you mean?" The worry came rushing back. She and Brevan wouldn't stop them. What to do?

"We can get ready for them, at least. Grandpa would want us to."

"What do you mean?"

"Come over here." Brevan knelt by Gven's locker, raised the lid, and fished out Grandpa's coin bag. "We can look after this, for a start."

"Brevan!" They were not supposed to go into Grandpa's chest. But, of course, he already had. "You took out Ryke's fee."

He nodded. "That's not all." He glanced to Gven, then whispered. "There's more. Grandpa's secrets. We must guard them."

"*Secrets?*"

"Another bag. With things in it—"

"What things?"

"I didn't have time to see. Here."

Brevan stuffed the coin bag in his pocket, and, dipping once more into the chest, brought out a second, larger bag and placed it in her cupped hands.

"Oh, how fine," she breathed. No cheap cloth pouch this, but a soft red leather drawstring bag. Worn shiny black at the outer creases, gold threads winking still fresh within the folds. The contents were heavy and their shapes felt intriguing. "Shall we peep?"

Brevan glanced to their grandfather. "Do you think we dare?"

Mylanfyndra pointed across the room.

They perched knee to knee in the narrow gap between their cots. There, Mylanfyndra untied the bag and shook it out.

CHAPTER 5

"O-oh!" Five gleaming, golden objects landed with a heavy chink into Mylanfyndra's lap. She took up the largest, a solid, shiny collar; wide at the throat, tapering toward a neat, rear hinge. On the throat clasp was a plain, polished stone bigger than an eye; a round black cabuchon.

"Let me see." Brevan took the collar and held it to the light. "Where did Grandpa get such a fine, rare thing?"

"Not off the mesa." Yet, if not, Mylanfyndra thought, then where else? The mesa was all there was. When Gven was young, he had circled it, to see where all the birds went come the glair, so he said. Six days, he came full circle back to the town, and all he saw was empty mesa on the inland side and wyrth off the cliffs. He criss-crossed the mesa several times after, but he never found the birds' refuge—or much else, for that matter. Only open tract and podlith.

"I know where the bag came from." Brevan pointed skyward, smirking. "The great Anlahr dropped it on top of Grandpa's hut. To pay for a broom, perhaps. Here," he went on hurriedly, as Mylanfyndra scowled, "let's put it on you." He slipped the collar around her neck, settling the stone at her throat, then leaned back, judging the effect.

For a moment, the metal felt cold and heavy. Then the sense of weight and coldness passed, and Mylanfyndra felt nothing at all. She fingered the collar's edge, to reassure herself that it was still there.

Brevan grinned. "It's a bit big, but it suits you well enough." He picked up a second object, a round disk, large and heavy.

"It's a medallion," said Mylanfyndra. The sort the Elders hung down their chests when sitting in the Moot, only larger, and much more handsome. Lacking a chain, it was the size of Brevan's palm, and almost as thick. Around the edge of the medallion was a wide, grooved border broken at one point by six small circles like flat beads in a row. Inside the border, a woman's head in left profile: straight nose, chin held high, wide brow capped by a shock of bushy curls that swept down in front like a collar. "Who's *that?* Here, Myl: take a look." Brevan handed the disk to Mylanfyndra.

Mylanfyndra took it, flipped it over, and exclaimed. *Anlahr!*

Caught in midflight, the figure's long hair streamed in the wind, and from the palms and heels shot jagged lightning spikes. The face was different from the woman's on the other side. Male? Or female? Could be either, except the figure wore leggings, and what female wore those? Whichever, this was the fire-spirit! "Your joke has turned to bite you, Brevan!" Mylanfyndra jeered, smiling fiercely. "That *is* Anlahr; the bag did fall from the air."

"Oh, really, Myl, I—" Brevan broke off, staring at her throat. "The stone—look at the stone!"

Mylanfyndra unclasped the collar, slipped it off. The stone was glowing like a warm ember, while in its depths licked tiny tongues of flame. "Oh, how lovely." She made to put the collar on again.

"Wait, Myl: you don't know what that means."

"It's all right," she said. "There's no harm or Grandpa wouldn't have it." She fastened the clasp, then took up the medallion again. "Gven said he saw Anlahr," she murmured thoughtfully. "What if he did more than that? What if they actually *met?*"

"Oh, come on, Myl."

"Then where else did these things come from, and who else can this be if not Anlahr!" She jabbed the figure with her finger.

Brevan pretended not to hear. He picked up two more objects: two thin bands like scraps of metal ribbon, and handed one to Mylanfyndra. Alike in size and shape, each was marked with symbols, similar, yet not identical. Being so thin, the gold bands bent easily. Brevan coiled his around his middle finger. "What are they, I wonder?"

"They could be bracelets—except they're much too small." Mylanfyndra's band barely reached halfway around her wrist.

"Rings, then?" Brevan held up his finger.

Mylanfyndra laughed. "Looks like a splint. You can't even bend your knuckle. I don't think so, Brev."

They restored the bands, set them down, and turned to the final object, a small tube the length of Mylanfyndra's hand. It was grooved, and encircled by thin gold bands along its length. "Here's a lid, I think." She tried to twist it off, but it would not budge.

Brevan was more successful. Lifting it off, he peered inside.

"What's in it?"

Shrugging, he handed it over. Mylanfyndra looked in, then held it upside down. A scatter of fine grains fell out, a mote-cloud dancing in the air. "Dust," she said as it drifted onto her lap. She brushed it off.

"What if it isn't, Myl? What if it's meant for something?"

"Like, what?" Mylanfyndra sneezed.

"Oh, I don't know. Like one of Ryke's powders. And now it's spilt all over the floor. Let's put these things back."

They gathered up the items and slid them into the bag. Brevan dangled the bag between them. "These things: what they are and where Grandpa got them is no one else's business, not even ours. They are his secrets, and we must hide them."

"Brevan! He'll have a fit!"

"He'll have a bigger one if someone finds them out. Someone, say, like Toova'ven-tuil," he added weightily.

Mylanfyndra looked around. "There's nowhere safe in here to hide them."

"I'm thinking of outside." Brevan stood and went toward the door.

In the *doft?* "The bag will be ruined."

"Not the doft. We stash it inside a dead 'lith branch."

"Oh yes . . ." Mylanfyndra smiled suddenly. "Let's do it." They took a lamp and cast around outside until they found the perfect place behind the hut: an empty vine case with twisting, hollow arms just wide enough to take the bag. After choosing the best limb, they stuffed it with 'lith shards an arm's length in to stop the hole. Then they shoved in the bag and sealed it in with more stone chips. At last, they stood back to survey their handiwork.

"No one would ever guess," Mylanfyndra said, holding out the lantern.

"Not even us, if we forget which is which, Myl," Brevan said.

True. "In that case . . ." Mylanfyndra scratched the limb with a mark like one she'd seen on the medallion. "There," she said in satisfaction. "We'll find it now."

That done, they went back in, fed the fire, and waited for the morning.

A loud knocking brought Mylanfyndra awake. She leaned across in the gray light and shook Brevan's shoulder. "Brevan, someone's outside."

Mylanfyndra went to the window, and stood on tiptoe,

craning her neck. A woman stood on the step; big, and round, and wide, in thick skirts and fringed shawl. Breath came from the shawl in quick, gray puffs, like wyrth. "Who is it?" Mylanfyndra called out, as if she didn't know.

"Toova'ven-tuil. Open up."

What could Mylanfyndra do but raise the latch and let the woman in? Toova pushed past, bringing in a swirl of bitter cold. Her hair stood out in wiry wisps around her shawl, her cheeks were flushed—and scratched, Mylanfyndra noted. The Tollwife slipped the shawl from her head and settled it about her shoulders, eyeing Brevan in distaste. "You: still standing by your bed in your nightshirt—did not Ryke tell you to meet me at sunup?"

Brevan frowned. "That he did not."

"No, you say?" Toova's brows went up. "After I distinctly heard him? I was down there at the appointed hour. But you were not. Never mind," she said, pushing past into Gven's corner, "I am here, which is what matters." She wrinkled her nose. "I smell liniment. That cost a good half-grat, at least. Did Ryke give physick, also? I'm sure he did," she went on, not waiting for an answer. "What was his total fee?"

The two children exchanged glances. "Two half-grats," Mylanfyndra said.

"Two?" Toova's brows came together.

"He said his fee was double after dark."

"Oh, did he?" Toova bent over Gven's still form, placing a hand on his brow. Then she looked up, without straightening. "Both of you—get dressed, hurry. You're to go down to meet the others who would come."

The children, stunned by the command, stayed still.

Toova straightened now, advancing. "If you do not dress and go at once, I'll put you out, just as you are."

They threw on their clothes, grabbed their coats, and fled.

"Ordering us out of our own house," Brevan muttered angrily, stomping along in front.

"We didn't even have a chance to look at Grandpa," Mylanfyndra huffed, stumbling after him. She scrubbed at her eyes irritably. What was Toova doing back there, alone in the hut, and Grandpa lying helpless in his bed? "I'm glad we hid the treasure," she said.

"*Treasure!*" Stopping in his tracks, Brevan fished the coin bag from his pocket. "We must also hide these."

"But where?"

Brevan shook out five coins onto his hand, and stowed them severally about his person. Then he handed the rest, in the bag, to Mylanfyndra.

"You hide this somewhere."

Mylanfyndra hung the pouch on her skirt sash, arranged her apron over it, then they moved on again, side by side.

"Why, Myl?" Brevan burst out. "Why all those people wanting to come up here? Grandpa will be so put out when he wakes up." He stopped again. "We could go back, say nobody came."

"And what when they do arrive, with Ryke? Toova will be furious when she finds we disobeyed."

"As Grandpa will be if he finds we didn't." Brevan smacked his hands together, making Mylanfyndra jump.

"Either way we lose: we're caught 'twixt Koos and Anlahr!"

They moved on down, until, near the bottom of the slope, they sighted a gaggle of women along with Ryke, struggling up the slope. One, a Widow Mayfy who lived behind the Moot Hall, called out, so what to do but go to meet them, as they had been told? In minutes, they were guiding the clumsy intruders up to the hut.

Toova waited in the doorway with bowls of hot mash.

"Take it." She held out the food to the children. "Over there, anywhere. Eat up. Then go find something to do. You can't come in," she added, blocking their way as they tried to go past. "You'll only get underfoot. Stand off— but not so far that you can't hear me," she added, letting the townsfolk through. "I'll call you in a while."

The children made no move to take her offering.

Toova set the bowls heavily down on the step. "Take it or leave it," she said. "I'll not stand here all day." She turned her back and went inside, shutting the door in their faces.

For a minute, Brevan and Mylanfyndra stood looking at the door. Then, without a word, they retreated across the clearing and sat down on a root tube, staring gloomily at the hut. Twin coils of steam rose from the mash bowls, up into the graying light.

"I'm not hungry," Mylanfyndra said.

"Me neither," said Brevan. "I feel bad."

Mylanfyndra felt bad too. Sick. Angry.

And afraid.

"What's happening, Brevan?" she murmured. Ryke, and Toova, and those other women: *what were they doing in Grandpa's hut?*

CHAPTER 6

For half an hour, they watched the hut door. Nobody came. Nobody went. Vague shapes crossed the window, to and from Gven's corner. Mylanfyndra kicked her heels against the tube. "What are they doing? What's going *on?*"

"I'm going to look." Brevan jumped off their perch and strode boldly to the door. But there he faltered, hand to the latch. Go on, go inside, Mylanfyndra urged silently. Instead, the door opened, and there stood Toova.

Brevan backed off a bit, then stood his ground.

"You," Toova said to Brevan. "And you, girl: come here. Come on," she added, as Mylanfyndra made no effort to obey. "Or do I fetch you?"

Mylanfyndra moved to join Brevan, dragging her feet.

Toova drew two small cloth bundles from behind her back, threw them out smartly. "Here . . . and here."

Mylanfyndra caught hers with a shock of recognition. Their good clothes, taken from their storage chest! Toova was surveying the cold mash bowls on the step beside her. "You don't intend to eat it?"

They shook their heads.

"So be it." Hands on hips, Toova surveyed them coldly. "Now: which of you holds Gven'bahr-brum's money?"

No answer.

"Willful, stubborn children," Toova said. "Tell—or do I search you?"

Mylanfyndra felt the pouch beneath her apron swelling by the minute.

"All right," Toova said, pushing off from the doorframe. She fixed her eye on Mylanfyndra. "We'll start with you."

Brevan spoke up. "I have it." He fished a coin from a pocket.

Toova took the coin, held it up between thumb and forefinger. "One half-grat? This cannot be all."

Making heavy weather of it, Brevan handed over another piece.

Toova tutted impatiently. "This could take all day. Listen, do you know what the Elders do with children who steal? You hand over the rest, or you go before the Moot."

"We do not steal! We are not thieves!" Mylanfyndra cried hotly. "That money is ours as well as Grandpa's!"

Toova looked sourly. "Children do not own money. Come: give."

"Why?" Mylanfyndra challenged, shocked at her own daring.

"There are debts to be paid. Ryke'ven-apoth awaits his

morning's fee, and—" Toova stopped, her neck flushing deep red. "What!" she cried, the flush spreading up over her face, "shall I stand here and argue the case with squits like you? Hand me Gven's money before I box your ears!"

With a deal of trouble, Brevan handed over two more coins, then displayed empty palms.

"Four half-grats?" Toova eyed Brevan suspiciously. "This is all?"

"We paid Ryke two last night," Brevan said.

"That tallies only six."

Brevan shrugged. "Our grandfather is not a rich man."

"Umm. Well." Toova was clearly unconvinced. She looked over her shoulder, called inside the hut. "Widow Mayfy! They're ready. Come out."

Mylanfyndra held up her bundle. "Why have you done this? Why do you throw our clothes at us?"

"You are going with Widow Mayfy."

They were to leave? With a townswoman they barely knew? "But—"

"No buts, girl. Take them, Mayfy," Toova said, as the widow stepped outside. Then the Tollwife went back in, shutting the door on them.

Mylanfyndra stood, outraged. Put from their own home! She crossed her arms firmly over her bundle. "I shan't budge," she declared. "Toova has no right. *No right!*" She blinked back gathering tears.

Brevan folded his arms likewise. "We demand to see Gven."

"Demand?" Widow Mayfy put her finger to her lips. "Nay. Children do not demand. Children do as they are told. Did Gven'bahr-brum teach you no manners?" She pointed to the hut door. "That's no place for you. The broom-maker is very, very sick. You must come with me now, as Toova said. There is no gainsaying her."

The children stayed put.

"Grandpa told us to stay home," Mylanfyndra insisted.

The hut door reopened and Toova poked her head around. "What! Still here?" She advanced off the step, forcing them backward. "You were told to go with Widow Mayfy, and go you shall—if I have to march you down myself."

"You can't make us!" Mylanfyndra cried.

Toova reached out, seized them both by the arms, and shook them until their teeth clicked, until Mylanfyndra dropped her bundle onto the doft. "Now," she said, releasing them with a push that sent them staggering. *"You will go!"*

Mylanfyndra snatched up her bundle and brushed it off. "We'll go, for Grandpa. But woe to you when he wakes up. As for shaking us—Gven has never treated us that way!"

"Pity," Toova said. "For you'd be better served now. Off with you."

Grimfaced, the children turned and walked stiffly away across the clearing, not looking back. Glassy dewbeads dropped from overhead; the soft, moist air smelled of doft. A good time, this hour of day; the hour when they usually set out with Gven to scour for stick and straw. But today they did not look around and breathe in deep to savor it all. Instead, they wound wordless through the podlithra, pulling steadily ahead of Widow Mayfy despite her calls for them to wait; that her way was blocked, that she had tripped on a root-tube, that her shawl was snagged on barbs. They reached the bottom of the slope, Widow Mayfy well behind.

Mist—the usual morning sort, flowed like a cold river across the open stretch 'twixt hill and town, hiding the distant houses so that only the chimneypots showed above the gray. As they turned toward the town, the sun cleared the mist, charging its upper layers with gold. Behind them, a firebird squawked and chattered, disturbed, no doubt, by Mayfy's clumsy blundering. Mylanfyndra gazed soberly into the dark, tangled slopes. How long before they went back up?

"It won't be long, don't worry," Brevan said, his breath curling. He'd caught her thought as usual.

"Don't worry?" Mylanfyndra turned on him. "This is a nightmare." And all her fault, she couldn't get that from her mind.

"At least we saved the money. And Gven's secrets, don't forget."

True. Mylanfyndra loosened, some. "Thanks to you. But what about Ryke's next fee?"

"There's a point. Four half-grats is not much. What when that gets all used up? Will Ryke stop giving remedy?" Brevan looked worried himself now.

"You wicked children!" Widow Mayfy came crashing out of the podlithra. She shook out her shawl, pulling off barbs, and resettled it about her shoulders. "Wait till Toova'ventuil hears that you left me behind! If you'd not get into worse trouble, you'll keep with me from now on."

They fell in beside her, walking in stubborn silence through the streets. Doors lay open to the morning air, bedding hung from windows; mats, on garden rails. One woman beat a rug against a wall, raising clouds of clay dust. A few streets along, a tow-haired girl of Mylanfyndra's age, sleeves rolled up, arms red and raw with cold, knelt over a stone trough beside the road, pounding out wet clothes. As they passed, a woman flew out of a nearby door. "Stop! I told you—fifty beats, then rinse!" she cried, and began to pummel the girl about the head and shoulders.

"Move on," snapped Widow Mayfy. "It's rude to stare."

"What a cruel mother," Mylanfyndra said, looking back. "The girl was doing her best."

"That's not her mother. The girl is geth."

"*Geth?*"

"An . . . house help."

Now the woman was dragging the weeping girl back into the house, leaving the clothes in the trough. "I wouldn't work for anyone who treated me like that," Mylanfyndra said.

"Geth have no choice. They go where they're sent."

"But what parent would send a child to a woman like that?"

"Parent?" Mayfy eyed them narrowly. "You don't know of geth? Truly, Gven'bahr-brum has spared you much."

"Spared us?" Mylanfyndra said.

"From what?" Brevan chimed in.

But Widow Mayfy was not of a mind to explain. "Come," she said. "The morning is half done; my bedding's not aired, my floors are not swept."

They walked on, until at last they reached Widow Mayfy's house—a run-down cottage in a back alley. Mayfy nudged them through the gate and up a broken path, across her front porch, and inside.

Mylanfyndra looked about curiously, never having been in an house before. Three doors led off the hall, two on either side, one ahead. This last opened on a kitchen. Back of the kitchen was a cold stone pantry smelling of sour pickles. "You'll sleep here," Mayfy said. "I'll find you mats to lie on. Drop your things over in that corner."

Sleep? They'd freeze on that floor. Mylanfyndra looked back to the warm kitchen. "We can lie by the hearth," she said. "We'll make no trouble."

"What, sleep in my kitchen? Did you ever hear the like!" Mayfy cried to the ceiling. "Now," she went on briskly. "Let me give you your tasks, for it's long past my breakfast time. You"—she pointed to Brevan—"fill a pail to patch the front path. The sack of stone mix is in the shed outside. Don't add too much water, or it won't set right. You, girl, come with me. You can shake out my bedding."

"Stone mix?" Brevan demanded. "Path? I know nothing of such work."

"Then learn, if you'd survive." Mayfy hurried Mylanfyndra across the hall into her bedchamber. The room was crowded with a huge fourposter. At its foot was a stepstool for climbing up; beside it, a commode. "Half an hour," Mayfy said. "When I have finished my breakfast, you'll have the bed aired, the slops emptied, and the windowpanes polished. Get moving," she urged, as Mylanfyndra stood. "There'll be more before this day is done."

CHAPTER 7

All morning long, the children toiled, Brevan patching the cracked front path and house walls; Mylanfyndra around the cottage. Noontime, delicious odors came and went, but no invitation to the kitchen.

Mylanfyndra thought of the spurned morning mash. Brevan must be hungry also, she thought, working so hard outside. As the afternoon wore on, she began to feel faint for lack of food. Never mind, she consoled herself. We'll have a good supper to make up.

Late afternoon, Mylanfyndra was tossing a pail of dirty scrub water off the back doorstep when she could stand it no longer. She set down the pail and ran around to the side of the house, where Brevan was splitting vine chunks. His hands were cracked and raw from the stone mix, Mylanfyndra saw. And his knuckles were bleeding. "I'm starved," she said. "How about you?"

Brevan wiped his forehead on his sleeve. "The same, just about."

"Hey!" Widow Mayfy called. "Back in, girl. And you—get on!"

"We are hungry!" Mylanfyndra called back. "And too weak to work."

"Agh!" the woman cried, disgustedly. "Come along in, then. I'll find you something, I suppose."

They went indoors to find the widow piling assorted scraps into a dish. While they watched, she stirred the scraps around, then scraped the resulting mess into two small bowls. "We're to eat *that?*"

"Be grateful, girl," Mayfy sniffed. "It's better than what most geth get." She packed them off into the pantry, and shut the door.

Mylanfyndra stared. "She called us geth."

"So? It means 'house help', and that is what we are, today."

"No." Mylanfyndra slowly shook her head. "It means something else." She went to sit with Brevan on the threadbare matting Mayfy had put down for them and dismally surveyed her bowl. Hard to see anything, the place was so dark, with the one small pane. And chill. She picked a piece of meat, bit it tentatively, then spat it out.

"Like what?"

"*I don't know!*" Mylanfyndra dashed away the bowl and covered her face.

"Hold on, Myl," Brevan urged. "When Gven wakes up, they'll be sorry!"

"What if he doesn't?"

Brevan took off his jacket, draped it about her shoulders. "You're shivering. Tell you what: tonight, when that old Mayfy's asleep, we'll go and look in on him. We can be there and back before anyone knows, mmm?"

At last she smiled.

But late that night, when they tried the pantry latch, it wouldn't budge. "She's locked us in!" Enraged, Mylanfyndra raised a fist to pound on the door.

"Hush, Myl!" Brevan seized her fist and held on. "Do you think that will get us out? Come on, let's go lie down."

"Lie down!" She pulled free. "How can you!" The strange, new roiling in her chest was back, and this time, it grew so bad she thought that she would burst. She felt Brevan's arm go about her shoulders.

"Come on," he said. "It's just for this one night."

The next morning, while they were dressing, Toova arrived.

"How's Grandpa?" asked Mylanfyndra, as the Tollwife hustled them bag and baggage out the door. "Are we going home now?"

"No," Toova said.

Brevan and Mylanfyndra cried out at once. "Why not? We shan't go back to Mayfy's!"

"You'll go where I say, and not another word!" Toova marched them to the Moot Hall, and up the steps. At the top, Mylanfyndra halted.

"Why are we here?"

"You'll see. Move on." Toova prodded them inside, under Koos and Anlahr, into a huge vestibule. The air was cold and clammy under the high rafters. "Smells like the Warren," Mylanfyndra whispered. Of stone and mold, and air that never reached the sun.

"Looks like it, too," Brevan answered, when Toova ushered them through the lobby, then up and down a maze of passages.

The Tollwife halted before a single door with an iron knob. "Wait," she said, and wagged a warning finger. She went through the door, closing it behind her.

"Why are we here?" Mylanfyndra said.

"Hush." Brevan put his ear to the door and closed his eyes. "There's talking. Toova, and a man. See if you can make it out."

Mylanfyndra bent to the lock.

". . . bring them, Toova'ven-tuil . . . I haven't all day to . . ."

Mylanfyndra straightened. "It's so jumbled."

"Sssst!" Brevan pushed her down again. "Keep listening!"

Mylanfyndra pressed her ear against the door, heard the man say ". . . state their case, Toova'ven-tuil, and be done."

Toova cleared her throat. "Last night, I heard . . . Gven'bahr-brum was taken ill. Knowing . . . numbers waiting to take his place, I took steps to forestall a general stampede to the hut."

"Take his place? Stampede?" Mylanfyndra echoed.

"Hush," Brevan said.

". . . reasonable step," the man was saying. "So then?"

"I went up . . . first light. I found Ryke'ven-apoth had told true."

"And?"

"When I arrived, I found the old man had expired."

Expired? Mylanfyndra turned to Brevan. "What's *expired?*"

". . . so I sent them with Widow Mayfy while we arranged for a Sending."

Sending!

Brevan clapped a hand to Mylanfyndra's mouth. Had she actually cried out? Her mind stood still but the voices went on.

". . . cannot convene a Sending for a mere broom-maker. How many more dead are waiting?"

"Two, dead these past two weeks, your worship. And they're bringing in a crewman from the Greater Podlithra—an unfortunate accident yesterday."

"Mmm. That would make four."

"And there is room for only three in the catacombs, your worship."

"Very well. Leaving Gven'bahr-brum up there is . . . seemly?"

"Oh, yes, your worship. It is still quite cold up in the podlithra. We can safely let him lie until the last minute."

"Very well. So now to these children. Would you—"

Mylanfyndra began to tremble, the trembling spread. She came up and leaned against the door. The door opened, she fell in; Brevan scrambled back.

"Eavesdropping, were you? That is no surprise," Toova hissed under her breath. She raised her voice. "Come right in, children," she said sweetly. "Daven-Elder will see you now."

Daven-Elder? Mylanfyndra grabbed Brevan's hand and hung on, edging past Toova into the chamber. Small, yet high-ceilinged, it was divided crosswise by a long table behind which sat a man in dark blue robes.

Toova pushed them forward to the table. "Stand straight," she murmured, and stepped back.

"So." Daven-Elder steepled his hands under his chin. "You know why you are here?"

The children shook their heads.

The old man sighed. "Sorry to say, Gven'bahr-brum is dead."

"You're wrong," Brevan said loudly. "He's only sleeping."

"The question now is what to do with you," Daven-Elder went on.

"We go home," Brevan declared. "Now."

The old man shook his head. "The hut is yours no longer. Nor the broom-maker's round."

"They are so!" Brevan cried. "It's our right according to the law, Grandpa said."

Daven-Elder raised a hand. "Gven'bahr-brum is not your grandfather."

"Not—"

"He is no kin at all."

CHAPTER 8

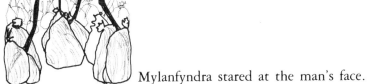 Mylanfyndra stared at the man's face. Gven not their grandfather?

"You mean you really didn't know?" Daven-Elder looked skeptical.

Brevan took Mylanfyndra's hand. "Gven *is* our grandfather!" he cried. "Breia, our mother, was his daughter. She died when my sister was born."

Daven-Elder shook his head. "Gven had no daughter. He never wed."

"Then where else could we have come from?" Brevan countered doggedly.

The Elder looked down his nose. "From time to time, young girls . . . give birth without husband to support them. You're not the first to be left out for others to rear, and I daresay you won't be the last. The puzzle is that you, boy, are a year older than your sister. Whoever it was managed to keep you hidden somehow. But you, girl, proved too much. When you were born, your mother discarded you together—not on a doorstep, as is usually the case. Sorry to say she took you up into the podlithra—on the eve of the glair."

Mylanfyndra gazed up, stricken.

"What mother would be so evil!" Brevan cried.

"Luckily for you, Gven'bahr-brum found you and rescued you—and nearly lost his own life in the doing. When he brought you into the Warren, we asked throughout, but none would claim you—and not even the Tollwife discovered who the mother was." The Elder sighed. "Of course, with no one to own you, you should have been declared geth, but Gven'bahr-brum sued to keep you. The Moot granted his suit, and here you are."

"Grandpa told us all about Breia," Brevan said doggedly.

"How she helped him make brooms, and kept house," Mylanfyndra added.

"Did he now." Daven-Elder leaned back. "And about your father, too? What of him?"

The children fell silent. The times they'd asked, the answer had always been the same. *"Nay, when you're older. . . ."*

"Tales, children. Just tales," Daven-Elder went on. "The fact is that once more you are geth."

"Geth are house help," said Brevan.

Daven-Elder shook his head. "Geth are nobody. The dispossessed. Out of its kindness, this town feeds and provides them with a roof." He leaned over the table. "Be grateful that you had a home if just for a while. Most geth children have only ever known the brug." He looked up. "Toova'ven-tuil: I would place my seal."

Toova went to the door and poked her head out. "Ho, there. Wax and parchment for Daven-Elder!"

A liveried runner brought a stick of red wax, parchment, and a lighted taper. Toova held the shiny red stick over the flame, dripping hot wax onto the parchment. Daven-Elder laid his medallion on it, impressing thereon his mark of office. When the wax had cooled, the Elder handed Toova the parchment. "The geth have left the brug already?"

"They went to work at dawn as always, your worship."

"Then these two go to Krels'im-brug. He's to mind them for today."

Toova hemmed. "So please your worship, they could work for Widow Mayfy. I did half-promise—"

"You had no right." Daven-Elder frowned. "Folk must take their turn for geth labor." The man climbed stiffly to his feet. "You are geth now," he warned the children sternly. "Remember that and no harm will come to you. Forget your place and you'll soon find what we do to those who set themselves above the law."

"Now," said Toova, the instant Daven-Elder had left the chamber. "We send you on your way."

"Where is the brug?" Mylanfyndra demanded.

"And who is Krels?" Brevan said.

Toova scowled. "Geth do not ask questions." She stuck her head into the passageway and called "Wess!" The liveried aide came running. "Two for the brug!" The Tollwife thrust the parchment at him, then turned to the children. "Try your wherefores and why-nots on Krels, and he'll soon

62

change your tune," she said, and walked away.

The children stood nursing their bundles, numb with the shock of it all.

"Well, come along," Wess said. "I haven't all day."

"Where is this brug?" Mylanfyndra burst out.

"In the warehouse quarter—not a place I like to go. Krels is custodian—not a man I'd like to have in charge of me—but then I'm not geth."

"Neither are we," Brevan said.

"Oh, no?" Wess bowed low. "Pardon. My ears are acting up today. If you'll permit, I'll call a carriage to run you home!" He gave them a shove along the passage. "Move, geth. You've taken up enough of the day!"

They stumbled down the Moot Hall steps, then away from the town that they knew. The streets grew meaner, and dirtier. Refuse littered the sidewalks, and choked the gutters. Then there were no more sidewalks, no gutters; and no houses either. Just long, low sheds; row upon row of them. Men lolled in doorways, sprawled on steps, calling insults as the party passed. Mylanfyndra lowered her head, conscious of their stares.

"Pay no mind," Wess said. "It's the way of warehouse-men."

Mylanfyndra was not reassured. "Are we nearly there?"

"Yes, indeed. In fact—ah!"

They came upon a derelict freight shed, with cracked walls and a sagging roof where the beams had buckled. This—their new home?

Wess rapped on the ramshackle door. "Krels'im-brug!"

Boards creaked, boots crunched over grit, and Wess leapt back as the door swung out and bounced against the frame. "What do you want?"

"Nay. It's what you've got: two new lodgers."

Krels spat out an oath. "We're full."

The aide pulled out Daven-Elder's seal. "This says you're not."

"Tcha!" Krels knocked it aside contemptuously. "As if there ain't enough kids in here already. How am I supposed to feed them, eh?"

"Come off it, Krels," Wess jeered. "With what the geth bring home at night—you live better than I do."

"That's a laugh. Change places, then. Here, I'm a-tiring of your company. Let me make my mark and git you a-gone."

Wess held the scroll while Krels rubbed a thumb in the dirt, then made a dusty smear under Daven-Elder's seal. That done, Wess rolled up the parchment and took off without a word.

The children stood by the sagging steps, bundles in hand.

"Well," Krels said. "What have you brought us, eh?" He reached out.

Mylanfyndra clutched her bundle tightly. "Just our clothes," she said.

"Let's see about that." Krels snatched Mylanfyndra's roll and shook it out, tumbling bodice and skirt, chemise and hose and the rest onto the grimy floor. "Bah!" he said in disgust. "Pick them up." Now he turned to Brevan. "You: shake out your stuff."

Brevan obeyed.

"All right," Krels went on, as Brevan bent to retrieve his things. "Now turn out your pockets, you first, boy."

Reluctantly, Brevan pulled out his pockets, one by one, until, at the last, his remaining half-grat piece fell out and rolled.

"Hah! Now we're talking!" Krels pounced, picking it up. He spat on it, rubbed it against his sleeve. Then he turned to Mylanfyndra. "You, girl. Your turn," he said.

Eyes down, Mylanfyndra showed her empty pockets, keenly aware of the pouch beneath her apron.

"Umph," Krels said, when she was done. "You lived with Gven'bahr-brum? I'd have said he was worth more than that."

"The Tollwife went through his things," Brevan said.

Krels nodded. "Well, keep the clothes." He pointed out across the yard. "Find a stick and follow me."

A stick? Mylanfyndra and Brevan exchanged glances.

"A vine-stake. Come on, come on," Krels snapped. "Hurry up. There's plenty lying about the yard. Find one and bring it inside."

They leapt to obey. Brevan found the best one, a broken lath about three feet high. Krels led them up the rickety steps and inside. Daylight striped the walls. Above the webby rafters, rag plugs quivered in the drafts. A clear space wide enough for two to walk ran the length of the shed to the far end. But to either side there was no room to tread. A forest of sticks leaned at crazy angles, sticks marking piles of bales and bundles; little hills or islands crowding the floor. Clay dust danced thickly in the air— air so stale despite the drafty walls that Mylanfyndra's stomach churned.

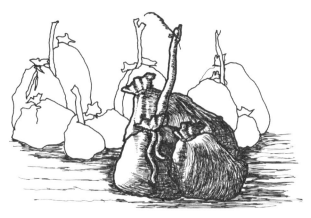

"See those?" Krels pointed to the sticks. "Them's stakes, see? They mark out folk's territory. Where there's a stake, the space is took. You better get that quite clear, if you don't want your heads a-busted. Now: find yourselves a space—if you can—and plant your stake. With luck, it's yours. "You, boy, what's your name?"

"Brevan."

" '*Brev*-an'," Krels mimicked. "Hoity-toity. Brev, you are, from now on. And you, girl? What do they call you?"

"Myl—" Mylanfyndra began, then stopped. If Brevan's name was too long, what would Krels make of hers?

"Mill? Haha! Grain mill? Wind mill? Or 'lith mill? Haha!" Krels slapped his knee, laughing hoarsely. "Well, Brev and Mill, find yourselves a spot—and like I said, keep off what's already spoken for. When you have found a spot—if you find one—stay put—and quiet. Hey, think of it this way: it's the last free time you'll ever have."

66

CHAPTER 9

They walked down the aisle slowly, looking from side to side.

"Krels is right," Mylanfyndra said, as they reached the far end. "There's not a space anywhere."

"Wait, look there." Brevan pointed. "Halfway along the back wall."

Mylanfyndra looked. "Maybe. Let's go see." They picked their way toward the gap around jumbled bags and bedrolls propping up their absent owners' stakes. There, the reason for the gap became clear: a hole in the floor big enough to fall through. A faint scratching came from underneath. A 'lith rat? Mylanfyndra tugged Brevan's sleeve. "I feel sick." That strange feeling again, a churning in her chest. If she didn't get out, she'd suffocate. They were almost to the door, when Krels called. "Not so fast: where do you think you're going?"

"My sister is taken poorly," Brevan called back. "She needs air."

"Oh, does she? Well, there's plenty in here—and if she don't like it now, just wait till later on!" He came out of the shadows, blocking their path. "You two have some adjusting to do, if you're to fit in here. All right, go on. Sit on the step for a spell. But make one move off it—and I'll be after you!"

They dropped their bundles in the open doorway and sat, looking gloomily out across the yard. "Brevan." Bad enough about Grandpa. Now something worse occurred. "If Gven isn't kin, if Breia never was, you and I might not be—" Mylanfyndra choked up. She couldn't bear to lose Brevan as well.

"Hey, come on, Myl. Finish what you started."

"You and I—we're not exactly alike."

"So?"

"Aren't brothers and sisters supposed to be?"

Brevan looked into her face. "We have the same eyes. Gray, and round, even if yours are a bit larger."

"But that's all. My hair's curly, yours is straight. Mine's brown, yours is black, just about. And my nose is short, yours is—well."

"Thanks, Myl," Brevan said. "I'm taller than you, quite a bit. But I'm a year older, too. Other kids in town, they're all different from one another in the same family. Like those in Mother Jever's house."

"But you can see they *belong!*"

"You can see we do, too, Myl. It's this way," Brevan went on, as Mylanfyndra stayed unpersuaded, "I likely look

68

more like one parent, and you, the other—though we'll never know which."

Mylanfyndra thought that one over.

"I must say," Brevan remarked after a bit. "Daven-Elder's story had a certain ring. The part about Grandpa finding us just before the glair. He always said how late he was getting down that year. How he nearly died."

"That was on account of meeting Anlahr."

"Oh, yes. Anlahr," Brevan said skeptically.

"And the golden treasures," Mylanfyndra cut in sharply.

"Hush, Myl." Brevan glanced behind. "I'd forgotten those. Good job we hid them, eh? But what now?"

"We can't stay here. This place is awful."

"Oh?" Krels stepped out onto the porch. "And where will you go, girl?"

Mylanfyndra swallowed. How much had the man heard? Krels seized her arm and yanked her to her feet. "Think you're the first geth with thoughts of running off?" He pushed her away. "Go on, try it. But you'll be back—if you're lucky."

"What do you mean?" Mylanfyndra said.

"You won't last long outside the town. How do I know? We've found what's left of others in the outer podlithras. At least, them as didn't get ashed in the glair." He leaned down close, so close that Mylanfyndra shrank from his foul breath. "If you still decide to scarper: you get flogged when they bring you back—and I'm the one as does it." He smacked his hands together with relish. "It's my job to keep geth in their place."

"You live here, then?" Mylanfyndra asked.

"Aye. Someone has to keep an eye on you."

"Then you're geth too?" she said, and promptly regretted it.

"Watch your lip, you! That's enough fresh air. Back inside and find yourselves a place!"

They finally found a spot in the rear left-hand corner, farthest from the door. The floor was ominously creaky, the walls were extra drafty. "But I feel safer with my back covered," Brevan said. "What do you think, Myl?"

"It's the only space, looks like." They dropped their rolls and propped their stake. Mylanfyndra looked around at the other stakes. Some were topped with some sort of token: a grimy ribbon, dried flowers, a firebird's feather.

She looked at their own stake, unadorned. What did she care? They wouldn't be here long enough to decorate. They sat, gazing around the darkened hall. Mylanfyndra tried to picture the place filled with people. Would they be rowdy? she wondered.

Brevan leaned over and put his eye to a slit in the wall. "It's only noon. What do we do the rest of the day?"

Mylanfyndra looked to the door. Krels still lounged against the frame, blocking the light. "We sit, I suppose," she said. "It feels strange, doing nothing, doesn't it?"

"Being hungry is worse," Brevan said.

Worst of all, Mylanfyndra found, one had too much time to think.

"There's to be a Sending."

"I heard."

"But Gven won't be there."

Brevan's head came up. "What are you saying?"

Mylanfyndra looked past him to the layered wall behind. "You know how he felt about those things."

"So? What do you propose we do?"

"I don't know. Stop it, somehow."

"Oh, Myl." Brevan sighed. "There's no way."

"So what will you do, then?" she snapped angrily. "Stand and watch them toss him off the cliff?"

Brevan turned abruptly from her. So Mylanfyndra turned from him, and there they sat, back to back, not speaking, like Koos and Anlahr.

Krels stretched and moved from the door, retreating into the gloom. At the movement, Brevan slid down on his back, and lay staring at the rafters. Round about now, thought Mylanfyndra, catching a slit of sky through the wall, they'd be heading for home, she and Brevan pulling the empty cart up the slope, Grandpa stepping behind.

"Don't, Myl." Mylanfyndra, crying silently, felt Brevan's arm steal around her shoulders as always, comforting. But this time she held herself quite stiff, not yielding an inch.

A shout cracked the peace. A commotion sprang up outside; men's voices raised angrily. More shouts, a scuffle. Brevan and Mylanfyndra scrambled up as Krels, muttering, clumped heavily onto the porch. "Here, here! Who's it fighting this time? Hey—break up—or I'll come and do it for you!"

"It were Levot! He took half my rations!"

"It were not! Beyjer grabbed Levot's box and his supper spilled all over. He had no right—"

"Get away! Beyjer was minding his own business! Levot started it!"

The babble grew louder, the voices, more numerous, until suddenly, there came crack, thud, then total quiet. Krels rapped out an order.

"In, all of you. Heffan and Croom—you two collect at the door."

A man and woman shuffled in and went to stand by two long tables on either side of the entrance. A moment later, people jostled their way inside, carrying pitchers and bowls, packets and boxes: leftovers from their workplace. They handed the food to the waiting couple, then moved on inside, scattering noisily to their stations. The children found each other's hand and held on.

The geth were coming home.

CHAPTER 10

"So many," Mylanfyndra whispered. Old, young. Women with babies on their backs and cradling infants. A man so bent with age his head was nearly to his knees. A one-legged youth, a woman helping him along—his mother?

"The middle's crowded," said Brevan. "But no one's coming our way."

"They will," Mylanfyndra said. "The pushy ones come first. They have the best spots. Stands to sense the folk out here will be in last."

Sure enough, the shed continued to fill from the center outward, until finally folk began to edge their way, pushing through with difficulty to the outer walls. A tall, thin youth approached, head down, shoulders stooped. His face was sickly, his eyes were dark-ringed, and his sparse, yellow hair scraped his shoulders. Seeming not to see them, he halted at the feathered stake and dropped, shutting his eyes in utter exhaustion.

A couple, too busy bickering to see where they were going, came next. To Mylanfyndra's relief, they settled several stakes away.

"I'm so hungry," Brevan said. "When's supper, do you think?"

"Who says we get any? We brought no food with us," Mylanfyndra said.

"Oh, you'll get something, don't worry," a voice piped up behind them.

They turned to find a girl—long, sharp face, sharp blue eyes, and wide mouth—kneeling by the stake capped with dried stoneflower blossoms. About her own age, as Mylanfyndra would judge. And familiar. "I've seen you before," she said, staring at the girl's short, tow-colored hair.

"It was yesterday," Brevan said. "On the way to Widow Mayfy's."

"Ah, yes." Mylanfyndra remembered now. "You were washing clothes!"

The girl screwed up her face in distaste. "Old Mother Yan's house. Pray Krels never sends you there! I know you—I seen you enough times with the broom-maker. What do they call you? I'm Ebbwe."

"I'm Brevan, *Brev,*" Brevan amended heavily. "And this is my sister, Mylanfyndra—Myl."

"Why are you in here? Are you geth now?" Ebbwe said. Just then, came the rattle of stick against iron pot, sparking a rush for the center aisle.

"Supper's up," said Ebbwe. "Follow me." The aisle was full, everyone was shoving toward the door. "That's where Krels doles it out," the girl explained. "Looks a proper battle, don't it? But it ain't, really. We all knows our turn. Come on."

"That's some task, sharing out the food," Brevan said, at Ebbwe's heels.

"It needn't be," Ebbwe retorted. "If Krels let us keep our own."

"Then some would have more than others, wouldn't they?" Brevan said.

Ebbwe laughed. "And Krels would get nothing. This way, he takes the pickings and leaves us the dregs."

By the time they reached the table, there wasn't much left: just two bites of mixed up mush and half a cup of cold broth each. Balancing cup and plate, Mylanfyndra followed Ebbwe and Brevan back to their corner. She was almost there when a foot shot out, tripping her. She staggered, caught herself—too late to save her supper. The broth went one way, the mush went the other, into a woman's lap, bringing on a shower of curses.

Quick as thought, Ebbwe kicked out at the protruding foot. There came an angry squeal and a head poked out. Another girl, dirty face, matted hair stiff as broomstraw.

"Ebbwe! Stinking brat! I'm going to tell!"

"You tell, I tell; tripping people up for spite!" Ebbwe snapped back.

Heads turned toward them. "It's all right, Ebbwe," Mylanfyndra said. "I didn't see. There's not much room, and it's so dark."

"She did it on purpose," Ebbwe said.

"Sure I did," the girl said nastily. "Now she don't get to eat, haha!"

Ebbwe turned her back. "Pay no mind: here." She thrust her own platter and cup at Mylanfyndra. "Hold these. I'll make her sorry!" Ebbwe lunged, but the girl ducked away and fled across the hall, laughing loudly.

"That was Vel; I should have warned you." Ebbwe slapped her hands together, as though brushing the girl off her skin. "She has no business here, she lives the other side. But don't worry. She'll pay. Meantime," she pointed to her plate and cup. "Have some of that. I don't need it all. I was somewhere nice today, with noontime vittles."

"Have some of mine too," Brevan said as they settled down in the small space between their neighboring stakes.

"Why did Vel trip me?" Mylanfyndra was deeply disturbed by the girl's hostility. "She's never even seen me before."

"You're new. You still look like proper folk. When you do get to look like geth, she'll pick on you some more to show you your place."

"Vel should worry. Brevan and I come last, so what's the quarrel?"

Ebbwe smiled. "You're quick," she said. "That's the way

76

the jobs go, too. We folk out here hardly ever get the good ones. I was lucky today, I told you. But I won't be again for ages. Eat up," she prompted Mylanfyndra. "I'm awaiting my share."

Mylanfyndra obediently scooped up a small portion of the mush with her fingers, and licked it tentatively. It tasted of nothing she knew.

"What do you think of this place?" Ebbwe asked, as Mylanfyndra handed back the plate.

"It's . . ." Mylanfyndra hesitated. What could she say? The brug was Ebbwe's home.

"It's awful," Brevan declared.

". . . and sad," Mylanfyndra ventured.

Ebbwe laughed shortly. "It's worse than sad. Worse than awful. It's hopeless," she said. "Some of us, like me, have been here since we were born. But others have had a real life. They know what it was like before the brug. Like Norj over there, see?" Ebbwe pointed to a small, quiet group a few stakes away: man, woman, and two small children. "He was a market gardener—had his own stall. Big house—I once scrubbed his floors. His harvest went bad two years in a row; blight. He lost everything. Now here he is, not a half-grat to his name. That man knows more than anyone in this town about growing things—yet this very day he was out laying street cobbles."

Mylanfyndra took a sip of broth. It was greasy and cold, not fit to drink. She swilled it around in her mouth: nowhere to spit it out . . . She swallowed, trying not to make a face, and handed back the cup.

"If you could pick, what would you do, Ebbwe?"

Mylanfyndra said, thinking that, as Ebbwe had spoken of growing things, there had been something in the girl's expression.

"Me?" Ebbwe looked surprised. She drank up the broth with relish, licked the empty cup, then set it down. "I went out of town once, right after the glair, up into the Greater Podlithra to clean for the 'lith crews. It was so pretty up there. The air was nice, and the whole place was sprouting. Have you ever seen the stoneflower stolons creeping over the doft? Of course you would have, up in the Lesser Podlithra. You'll likely think it nothing special. But me—" She broke off, sighing once more. "There were other plants, too. Feathery grasses that last for a day. They shoot from the doft in the morning, flower at noon; then puff out their seeds to the stars. By dawn, they're gone and the next lot are poking through. If I could, I'd have a little plot, and grow things." Her eyes lit up. "Sometimes I dream of a place where things have time to get tall, and old; where they're not burned to ash every year. Some dream, eh?" She gathered up her empty cup and plate. "Let's take our things back, and we'll go outside."

"I thought we weren't allowed." Mylanfyndra craned over the crowd and saw a steady stream of folk going in and out the door.

Ebbwe grinned. "There's one place you can go. And it's now—or never!"

Returning their plates and cups to the tables by the door, Ebbwe led them out and around to the back of the brug. Here, the children found, were two smelly bathhouses, one for men, the other for women. "But we don't wash too much until the nights gets warmer," Ebbwe said, as they left Brevan and went into the women's bathhouse. It was foul inside. A line of privies down one wall, a trough down the other, and the floor between, slick and slimy.

Mylanfyndra swished her hands in the scummy trough, splashed her face one-two, then hurried back outside with Ebbwe to find Brevan waiting, gazing across the darkened yard.

Mylanfyndra expelled the stink of the bathhouse through her nose and filled her lungs with cold night air. "How long can we stay out here?"

"Don't even think it," Ebbwe said. "Don't you like the warm?"

"Ye-es, no," Mylanfyndra said awkwardly. "I can't bear to be shut in."

"Well you'll have to put up with it for now. Krels will be watching you closely until you settle. Listen." Ebbwe looked about, then lowered her voice. "Watch out, Krels has spies. Come on, let's go. It's lockup time."

"We get *locked in?*" The stifled feeling came back, just as in Widow Mayfy's pantry. Suddenly, Mylanfyndra had the urge to run, feet skimming the ground, arms pumping, propelling her along. Her throat tightened. Her breath came fast and short. She was going to suffocate!

"It's the law," Ebbwe was saying. "Our good townsfolk don't want geth on the loose. Especially at night. But there's a way—" She broke off.

"That's all right. You hardly know us," Brevan said.

"Oh, I want to tell you. I know I can trust you." Ebbwe moved closer. "There is a way to get out at night. But I can't show it to you until after things are quiet—now don't get all excited, or Krels will want to know why," she warned, then led them back inside.

The wait seemed long. Mylanfyndra was so tired, she kept nodding off. But at last, when all had been quiet for a while, Ebbwe nudged them up. She led them along the back wall step by careful step, past crumpled sleeping bodies, then stopped. "Careful: mind the hole."

The hole in the floor that they had seen that afternoon. Mylanfyndra thought of the scratching noises. "We're to go down there?"

"No," Ebbwe said. "The place is right by it, in the wall."

Edging closer, Mylanfyndra could just make out Ebbwe groping about where the wall joined the floor. Presently, Ebbwe looked up. "Here, feel this." She guided their hands to a ridge of wall jutting out farther than the rest. "Got that? Now watch." Grasping the ridge firmly, Ebbwe pulled. A chunk of wall slid out with a faint grating noise, leaving a horizontal slit just wide enough for a child to squeeze through. "Follow me," she said, and wriggled through the hole. Brevan followed, then Mylanfyndra.

Without a word, they crept away out of earshot, to the edge of the yard. "We'd best go no farther."

Mylanfyndra stood, gratefully breathing in the moist night air. She could feel the tightness easing in her chest. "Aaaaaah, I could stay out all night," she said.

Ebbwe shivered. "Not me."

"How long could you stay out before getting caught? I mean, how long does everybody sleep like that?"

"Krels bangs the pot one hour before sunup. We get bread, then everybody lines up and he unlocks the door."

"And then what?"

"There's a crowd outside waiting for geth labor."

Mylanfyndra glanced to Brevan. "So who's to know if you just stayed out here and pretended you'd come from inside?"

"Didn't you hear me before? Krels has eyes—and ears—all over. You're not there when he bangs that pot—he'll know."

"An hour before dawn," Mylanfyndra murmured. She thought of the podlithra, empty, silent. Gven, lying alone in the hut. "Let's go back in," she said suddenly.

Ebbwe grinned. "I was wondering how long before the cold finally got you. All right, come on. But, hey—if you should come out any time and get caught—"

"We won't," Mylanfyndra said.

CHAPTER 11

"Brevan?" Mylanfyndra said, as soon as Ebbwe had gone to her own stake. "I know what to do for Gven."

Silence.

"Brevan, listen. We take him to the Grandpa Grove and hide him in his favorite place. Tonight."

"Myl, we couldn't possibly. Besides, there isn't time."

"We have hours. All right, don't come, then," Mylanfyndra said, when Brevan didn't answer. "I'll go alone."

They slipped through empty streets, across the open tract to the foot of the podlithra, and up to the hut. They stood, so still that Mylanfyndra could hear the blood squeaking in her ears. Nothing moved, not even the air. They crept past the broom cart to the hut door, raised the latch, then opened the door a crack. Familiar smells curled out around them, like an old scarf. Brevan found the tinder box, lit a lamp, and took it to Gven's corner.

"Grandpa." Nothing—*nothing* could have prepared Mylanfyndra for this! The old man laid out, arms folded across his chest, his face, his whole body swathed from head to toe, ready for the Sending. Beside the cot, a bale of white cloth, folded, waiting: the shroud. "Oh, Brevan, clear his face."

Brevan parted the bindings, revealing a peaceful brow, eyes closed in . . . sleep? Mylanfyndra's hope leapt. Why, she thought. The fever's gone, he looks so rested. She touched her fingers to his cheek, recoiled. "He's cold, so cold."

Brevan shifted uneasily beside her. "Myl. We must get on."

They readied the broom cart, propped open the door. "I'll take Grandpa's shoulders," Brevan said. "You take his feet."

They tugged on him, lifted him an inch or two, then let him fall back onto the cot. The weight of him, and he so slight! "We can't do this, Myl," Brevan said. "We're not strong enough."

"Yes, we can," Mylanfyndra insisted. "If we really brace ourselves."

They tried again, Brevan locking his arms around Gven's shoulders, cradling his head against his chest. "Ready, steady—*go!*" They made for the door, hurried through, and dropped Gven awkwardly onto the cart. He didn't fit, quite; the old man's head lolled at one end, the legs hung down at the other. Brevan tried the shafts. "This isn't going to work; we'll never make it, Myl."

"Yes, we will—and must," she said firmly. "I'll get his things." Still in Gven's locker, thank goodness. She put his good clothes, winter cap and boots, and festive drinking cup onto his shawl and rolled them all into a bundle. She took one last look around, put out the lamp, then went out, closing the door behind her.

"Here." She laid the bundle in the cart beside Gven. "Let's go."

"Wait," Brevan said. "We're forgetting the treasure." He retrieved the pouch from its hiding place and put it with Gven's pile, and now they began to climb, hauling the cart after them.

Halfway up the first stretch, Mylanfyndra looked down with horror on Gven's body. "Stop! Stop! He's slipping!"

They wedged the wheels, and shifted Gven about, trying to fit him in more securely, Mylanfyndra half-sobbing with the strain of it. To treat Gven thus! It scarcely bore thinking of—but what else to do? "It's so hard with all those wrappings," she snapped, to mask her distress.

Brevan seized his chance. "And we won't make it up that last incline, Myl. The cart's so heavy. I think we ought to take him back."

"No!' Mylanfyndra turned on him fiercely. "Do you want him thrown off that cliff?" she cried, then went on, lowering her voice. "We've come this far, we have to finish. Let's go!" She hauled on her shaft with renewed effort leaving Brevan no alternative but to follow suit. Slowly, they moved off, making their way in fits and starts up slopes that seemed steeper than Mylanfyndra remembered. Somehow, they made it to the top.

Mylanfyndra leaned against the cart, hot and breathless.

"Now what, Myl?" Brevan was waiting, reluctant to make the first move.

She walked over to Grandpa's bole. "We have to stop up the base," she said, peering in. "You get inside while I find 'lith shards."

Brevan clambered through the side hole and let himself down into the hollow caisson. There, he braced his feet against root-tubes, and, taking the shards as Mylanfyndra found them, jammed them in the gaps until the floor was all filled in. "Now what?" he said, when they had finished. "How are we going to lift Grandpa inside by ourselves?"

"The same way we got him into the cart."

"But he won't fit, Myl."

"We'll curl him on his side," Mylanfyndra said. The way she liked to go to sleep.

"I suppose. But we'll need to loosen these bindings first."

By the time they had slackened the cloth strips, Gven's head was bare. "I'm glad," Mylanfyndra said. "He looks easier now." She brushed back his hair with her fingers. "Grandpa, forgive us, but we know you'd want this," she whispered, then climbed inside the bole while Brevan hoisted Gven's shoulders high enough for her to catch. Together, they hauled him up through the hole, then lowered him inside, curling him into the hollow space.

Grandpa.

When she was very small, Gven tucked her in at night, slipping the edges of her blanket firmly under the mattress to keep out the drafts. Mylanfyndra made a pillow of his jacket, slid it underneath his head. Then she shook out his shawl, and laid it over him, tucking it under all around. "Sleep well, Grandpa," she said, then bending awkwardly, she kissed his brow as he had always kissed hers.

They piled the rest of his clothes at his feet, set the cup and knife by his head, and climbed back out. Mylanfyndra leaned shakily against the 'lith bole. "We did it, Brevan. We saved Grandpa from the Sending!"

Brevan peered in through the hole, surveying their handiwork. "I didn't want to. I was scared we'd be caught. But now I'm glad. He would have hated it, and he looks so peaceful here."

"And private, with his things around. . . . " Her voice

went wobbly. She shut her eyes, hard. She wouldn't cry, she wouldn't! "You know what?" she said. "However bad things get, Grandpa will be here. We can come and be with him, and breathe the good air." She took one last look, then together they piled large 'lith shards behind the hole, sealing him in—and the rain out.

Mylanfyndra stood back to survey their handiwork. "What do you think?"

"It's fairly fine," he said, looking to the sky, and Mylanfyndra knew that he was getting nervous again. They turned to leave—only to find once more that they had forgotten to enclose the strange treasures. No time now to unseal the podlith and put them in after Gven!

"Don't worry," Mylanfyndra said quickly. "We'll stow them nearby." Down the next bole in the podlith circle. Now they fled back down the slope, and, leaving the broom cart by the hut, hurried back to the brug.

They paused just inside, standing quite still, looking and listening. Everything seemed the same. Edging stealthily back to their corner, they passed Ebbwe and the pale youth, barely discernible in the darkness. Reaching the safety of their island, they got down quietly and prepared to sleep. Mylanfyndra curled up on the bare floor, feeling pleased at their success. But barely had she gone to sleep, it seemed, when Krels banged the pot and everyone was stirring.

CHAPTER 12

"Cold, ain't it?" Ebbwe said cheerily, as they joined the bread line. "Never mind, the sun will soon be up."

"Hurry!" Krels called from the porch. "There's folk a-waiting for you."

Clutching chunks of bread, the children moved out with Ebbwe. Geth crowded the porch, surrounded by strangers wrapped against the chill.

"See that fellow in the fur hood?" Ebbwe murmured. "He's a mean one. Ironmonger. Needs a strong arm to shift his stock. Notice how the men shrink back when Krels looks at them?"

A tall, thin lady hurried up, in cloak and feather. "Krels, Krels my good man. I trust I'm not too late, that there is still someone suitable?" She pressed something shiny into

Krels's hand. Two geth women rushed forward, jostling each other, vying for the lady's eye.

"That's Mistress Ather," Ebbwe said. "A good, motherly sort. She wants someone to mind her children."

"It is almost our turn," Mylanfyndra said apprehensively as the geth crowd dwindled. "I wonder where Krells will send us."

Ebbwe went to work on a market stall. Brevan walked away with a burly brickmaker. Mylanfyndra went to beat linen in the public laundry, a long, narrow room filled with lines of wash troughs. The walls ran wet, the floors were treacherously slick, the rafters dripped unceasingly; no sign of daylight. The noise of slapping and splashing and shrill gossip was deafening. Mylanfyndra picked up a sheet, dropped it. Like a shroud, it was.

"Courage, geth," Mylanfyndra's neighbor said, a woman with chapped and shining face. "The first day's always hard. But you'll get used to it. And what's more, you'll be resting tomorrow. We have a Sending."

"Sending?" Another woman set her linen down. "Who's dead, then?"

"Who cares, as long as it ain't us!"

Tomorrow! Mylanfyndra leaned on the trough. Were they fetching Gven?

"Here," her laundress said, taking up Mylanfyndra's sheet and shoving it at her. "You get down to work, or I'll report you!" She turned to the others and shrugged. "Geth," she said. "What more can you expect?"

Noontime, Mylanfyndra was given sweet root to chew,

and a cup of water to swallow. Then she was back, bending over wet cloths, slapping, wringing, dunking; slapping, rinsing, all afternoon. By the time she was dismissed, she was almost too tired to walk, and she had no strength left in her hands. Outside, the late afternoon air struck chill and shivers feathered through her overheated body, and the trudge back to the brug seemed to take so long, much longer than in the morning. Brevan sat by their stake, watching the door. As she approached, he came to meet her. "You look awful. What happened?"

"You don't look so grand yourself," Mylanfyndra answered. "Have you heard? Tomorrow—"

"—there's a Sending." Brevan pulled her down. "Toova was here. She asked Krels about us. Where we were last night. But she wasn't satisfied. She said to tell us she'll be coming back tonight."

After supper, the children were walking from the bathhouses, when Mylanfyndra halted. Toova—with Krels, watching folk in and out.

"Hey," Ebbwe said. "What's she doing here?"

Krels caught sight of them, beckoned. "Here, you two. You—" He jabbed a finger at Ebbwe. "Inside."

"Now, Krels," Toova said. "I'll question them." The Tollwife folded her arms. "You will tell me: where is Gven'bahr-brum?"

"Don't answer!" Krels commanded. "The woman's raving."

Toova rounded on him. "Krels'im-brug, the broommaker's disappeared as these two well know—and whoever helped them."

"And that's me, that's what you're saying. You're out for my hide, to save your own," Krels said heavily.

"It's plain to anyone with sense, you foolish, greedy man," Toova countered. "The broom-maker's things are missing, also. It's clear that these two bribed you to give them a hand." She fixed the children sternly. "Why did you move Gven'bahr-brum from the hut? And where have you put him?"

Mylanfyndra and Brevan turned to each other in a show of mute confusion.

"Very well," Toova said. "I shall go to the Elders. This place shall be searched, and they shall question you."

"Go ahead, make a fool of yourself," Krels sneered. "See how far it gets you. Everyone knows how I bar the door at night. Ain't nobody can leave here till morning. And what would these innocent children want with a dead old man? As for the thievery: you're the one they'll fault, leaving that hut untended. And if you want to find the missing things—look closer to home. There ain't no thieves cage in the market place for nothing."

Toova glared. "You defy me, Krels'im-brug. I'll make you pay."

"*Defy?*" Krels's anger flared. "Who do you think you are? You ain't over me. Go on, bring me up before the Moot, and you're the one as will be sorry! Now, get. It's time for me to bar the door."

"Very well," Toova said quietly. "I'll go for now. But I'll be back."

Ebbwe was waiting. "What did Toova want?"

"She accused us of being out last night," Mylanfyndra said.

"Oh!" Ebbwe's eyes widened. "And what did you say?"

"Nothing," Brevan said. "Krels spoke for us."

"He *what?*"

"To save himself," Mylanfyndra said. "We can't explain right now."

Ebbwe whistled, then bent close. "*Did* you go out . . . after?"

Just then, there came a faint rustling from Ebbwe's pile. Ebbwe sprang, then turned back with a shrug. " 'Lith rats. They're all over," she said. "Let's talk of other things. Did you know we have a break tomorrow? There's to be a Sending."

"Yes," said Brevan. "We know."

The next morning, Krels lined them up and marched them to the cliff edge to witness the ceremony. Mylanfyndra and Brevan closed their eyes and covered their ears, shutting out the caterwauling. All night she had turned and turned about, mulling over Toova's threats until by dawn she was really frightened. But now? She thought of Gven curled peaceably among the podliths. "I don't care; it was worth it," she murmured, squeezing Brevan's hand, and by his answering squeeze she knew that he took comfort likewise.

CHAPTER 13

Each afternoon, the children returned to the brug more tired than the day before. By the week's end, they fell on their island and lay, as the pale youth did each day. His name was Fos, which meant ember: an apt name for one whose spark was long since spent.

"Poor Fos," Ebbwe said. "He's been like that since Harv died in the last glair. Harv was his friend, you know. He was . . . where you are now."

Mylanfyndra shifted uneasily. Not her fault Harv was gone, that she was in Harv's space. Now she recalled the Sending in the Warren, three bodies: two large; one smaller, unnamed, unmourned. "Did Harv have a Sending?"

"You saw it?" Ebbwe lowered her voice. "I thought Fos would try to follow. He's still dragging on, and nothing I do can shake him out of it. I—I think he just wants to die."

"Who wouldn't, in this place?" Brevan said.

"Oh, no! Not you too!" Ebbwe groaned. "Hold on. You'll be fine once you get used to it. This is the hardest time."

A small rock flew from nowhere, landed by Mylanfyndra's foot.

"That Vel!" Ebbwe leapt up. "Keep to your side, or I fetch Krels!" she shouted.

Vel sprang from her hiding place, waving her arms triumphantly. "Get you next time!" she cried, and took off.

"She never gives up," Mylanfyndra said, picking up the rock and examining its sharp edges. "Will she ever stop baiting us?"

Ebbwe shrugged. "It depends on who's behind her."

"Behind her?"

Ebbwe looked around. "There's talk of bad blood 'twixt Krels and Toova. That night you first came here—he was out to save his skin. But that don't mean he ain't suspicious. He's watching you, and maybe Toova's watching you, too. And Vel would gladly spy for both."

The next day, on her way back to the brug, Mylanfyndra found a large, handsome *parvi* shell beside the road. Save for a nick where some bird had plucked out its fat inhabitant, the shiny, purple shell was quite intact. Mylanfyndra retrieved it and laid it on Fos's pile. Soon after, Fos arrived back, was just about to cast himself down, when he saw the shell. He picked it up, examined it, then glanced around, puzzled. Mylanfyndra caught his eye and nodded, smiling. A brief spark lit his pale face, like a flash of sun on a showery day. Bowing his head in thanks, he hung it on his stake tip with the feather, where it leaned like a ceremonial cap.

"Hey!" Ebbwe arrived. "That's a fine shell, Fos. Where'd you get it?"

Fos looked toward Mylanfyndra, threw her one more quick smile, then he sat, back turned, hunched over.

"That was nice of you," Ebbwe said. "He's really touched."

Mylanfyndra slept badly that night, waking to the slightest noise. Her muscles ached, her skin was dry and cracked. She tried sitting up, and out of nowhere a shadow loomed. Krels, of course. It was uncanny these days, how quickly he appeared. She lay down, fast, and closed her eyes—too late. He nudged her ribs with the toe of his boot. "Why aren't you asleep?"

When she didn't reply, Krels dug harder. "Answer when I speak to you."

Mylanfyndra sat up again. "I don't feel well."

"Hah! You want me to fetch the apothecary? Listen." Scattered noises were coming from all over. Even in the middle of the night folk coughed and groaned and babies fretted. "Nobody's well in this place; it's a part of living here. Whilst I'm about it . . . " He crouched beside her. "Did you do the things that Toova said?"

"Did *you?*"

"Why you—" Krels raised a fist, looked around, then lowered it. "The old man's belongings what *somebody* took—was there anything of value?"

"How would I know? Grandpa never let us in his private locker."

"O-ho, of course not," Krels leered. "Listen, I tell you this much: you two puzzle me mightily. Squits like you— you ain't moved that old man on your own, she knows that.

95

I knows that. Now if, like she says, you did get somebody to help you, and if you did take Gven's stuff, I could help keep her off your back—if you made it worth my while. What do you say?"

Mylanfyndra said nothing.

"Oh well." Krels got to his feet. "I ain't in no hurry. And you ain't going nowhere. Talk it over with your brother, eh?" he said, and moved off.

"I was hoping it had all passed over," Brevan said when Mylanfyndra told him the next morning.

"Me, too. What bothers me is where's that enquiry over Grandpa? Why isn't Toova still kicking up a fuss? It doesn't seem right, somehow."

Brevan shrugged. "You heard Daven-Elder call Gven a mere broom-maker."

"You mean he's not important enough?" Mylanfyndra frowned. "Could be. But I'd say messing up their Sending was a serious matter, regardless of a body's rank, Brevan."

Whatever the reason, the enquiry never took place. Yet Mylanfyndra stayed uneasy, sure that Toova and Krels would not let the matter go like that. For weeks after, Mylanfyndra kept on guard, sensing that she and Brevan were watched, in and out the brug.

Spring burgeoned into early summer. Seed and root swelled, grew, ripened into harvest. Several times, the children were sent to dig up the root crops in the market gardener's clay plots: backbreaking toil, under a blistering sun. As the harvest dwindled, talk turned to summer's fiery climax: the coming glair. Up in the podlithra, the firebirds began a miraculous transformation, a process Mylanfyndra would sorely miss this year. As the glair approached, those plump, clumsy birds lost their fat, round shape and twin buds swelled on their backs. She had loved to watch the

buds grow into stumps, the stumps spread into what looked like webbed hands. As the days passed, the nascent wings took on a cover of bright red down; soft, and fuzzy. As the weather warmed, the fuzz shed and quills came in, scarlet, and yellow, and vermilion. Still grounded, the birds would lift and spread these feathered growths, flapping them unceasingly—to strengthen them, Gven said. To Mylanfyndra, it seemed each year that for all the changes, the birds would never rise; that they were too heavy and their wings, too weak . . .

Mylanfyndra sighed. True, she would miss this yearly miracle, but just now she was too tired to care. Tired and dispirited to see Brevan come home worn down every night—and she feeling just as bad. It got so that not even Ebbwe could cheer her, so that when she lay down to sleep at night in that hot, close shed, she hoped she wouldn't wake up. At last, she could bear it no longer. "Brevan," she said, as they settled down for the night. "I'm going to see Grandpa. Coming?"

"But we'll be caught."

"So what? I'm going, so will you come with me?"

"Have I a choice?" Brevan answered.

No wind, not the slightest draft, blew through the sultry streets. Even their light footfalls sounded loud in Mylanfyndra's ears. They cleared the town, crossed the open space to the foot of the podlithra, and stood gazing up into the tangle, breathing in the old smells.

Home.

Looked different somehow, thought Mylanfyndra. The bank seemed steeper; the tangles, denser. Closed.

"It's changed," Brevan said.

"No-o," Mylanfyndra answered slowly. "It's us."

"Let's go back."

"To that place?" Mylanfyndra took Brevan's hand, tugged it lightly. "Let's go on . . . please?"

"All right. Shall we see the hut first?"

"What about the new folk?"

"They'll be sleeping. Can't hurt just to go by," Brevan said.

Mylanfyndra wasn't so sure.

"Oh, look," said Brevan. "They've painted the broom cart."

"So they have." Red? Or brown? It was difficult to tell in the dark. "They've painted the door, too."

"They've cleared more vine," Brevan added, as they went around the back. "Lucky we moved Grandpa's treasures." That podlith was quite gone.

So many changes, thought Mylanfyndra with a pang. It had been a mistake to come, just as she'd suspected. She pressed her fist against her chest.

"What's up, Myl?"

"Nothing," she said. "It's just . . ." She tapped her breastbone. "I feel funny in here, as though I'm going to burst. It started when Grandpa took ill. I thought—"

"Me, too, Myl!" Brevan burst in. "Me, too! I've been so scared."

"You never said."

"Neither did you. Maybe it's a kind of ailment, Myl," Brevan said uneasily.

Mylanfyndra took his hand. "Let's move on."

They began to climb. At every step, Mylanfyndra's heart—and feet—grew lighter. At the crest, she let go Brevan's hand and ran to Gven's bole. "Grandpa." She laid her cheek against the rough stone casing.

Brevan turned away, gazing up at the stars.

Mylanfyndra went to join him. Without intending it, she spread her arms wide, then, gazing upward, she began to turn about, slowly at first, then faster, until the stars began to blur. Her head was light; her body—her whole being was light and getting lighter. As though at any moment she would simply rise from the doft and float into the air . . . She closed her eyes, feeling pleasantly giddy. "It's almost as if I could *fly,*" she murmured.

Gentle airs stirred about her body, lifting her hair, fanning her cheeks. Oh, to stop still, caught in that moment! Why, she could scarce feel the ground beneath her feet. . . .

Brevan's quiet voice cut across her dreamy state. "Myl."

Mylanfyndra opened her eyes.

Brevan, pointing down.

"Brevan?"

Face-to-face they were, indeed—and floating light as stoneflower seed, thirty feet above the doft!

CHAPTER 14

They landed with a bump, and lay, winded. The lightness was gone, and the strange feeling in Mylanfyndra's chest. She raised her head. Brevan was lying still, face down. She glanced across to Gven's grave.

"What happened?" Mylanfyndra dug Brevan in the ribs. Even birds did not rise with the air, but flew by beating their wings. "Brevan, folk don't rise." Only spirits. Like Koos and Anlahr.

Brevan sat up, rubbing his eyes.

"Perhaps it's this place," Mylanfyndra went on. "You know, being here with Grandpa, and all."

"No, Myl. Grandpa's gone. Dead. It's something else." He scrambled to his feet. "And whatever it is, I don't like it. I'm getting out of here!"

Later, waiting for sleep to come, Mylanfyndra relived the

miracle on the knoll. She had felt so light and so fine. *Right.* She could still feel the airs against her skin, the surge of elation; the lightness bearing her up. . . .

The next day, not one word did she and Brevan speak of it. Nor the next day, nor the next. In fact, they didn't speak much at all.

"You two are quiet," Ebbwe said at last. "Have you had a spat?"

"Not exactly," Mylanfyndra said.

As the next few days passed, the desire grew to return, to stand on that place where the impossible, the unthinkable had happened. Desire became need, an undeniable urge. "I'm going back," she whispered to Brevan one night as they lay down to sleep.

"Myl, don't. You can't."

"I can, and will. Just try to stop me!"

Mylanfyndra stood in the podlith circle, waiting.

Nothing; no surge in her chest, no burst of energy. She went to Gven's 'lith bole, laid her face against it. "I'm still glad I came, Brevan."

"The air's good," he conceded cautiously.

Mylanfyndra strode back to the hill crown. How grand it had felt, to close her eyes, and spread her arms, just so, and . . . simply rise.

"Myl." Brevan sounded warning. Mylanfyndra opened her eyes to find her feet inches from the ground. She landed with a little bump. Which had done it? Closing her eyes? Spreading her arms? Turning? Or all of them together? Excitedly, she began them all again.

"We mustn't, Myl. It's not natural."

"Suit yourself." Mylanfyndra shook him off and closed her eyes.

"Myl, don't!"

"Mustn't! Don't!" Mylanfyndra mocked. She reopened her eyes. "You begin to sound like Toova! Rising's not bad. It's wonderful, and quite special. And our strange, new feeling is a part of it."

"You think?" Brevan looked uncertain. "Even so, I'll still wait here."

Mylanfyndra turned from him, closed her eyes, and tried to recreate her peaceful, happy feeling. She took a deep breath of night air, let it out slowly, then, spreading her arms, she thought how light, how lovely, to rise and play the currents above the hill. There! Brevan called out something, but this time she paid no heed. This time, she felt the weight leave her body, felt herself lifted by the airs. Higher, higher, feeling colder currents now. *Grandpa, see: I'm flying!* She looked down. Brevan was on his feet, a speck on the bald hillcrown, arms akimbo, pale face upturned. She risked a wave. The gesture sent her careening, tumbling out of whack. Hands pricking, she steadied herself, thrust off into the head wind, and cut a wide arc. How? she thought. How had she known the way to steady herself, to catch that particular draft? Truly, this was a gift of the spirits! "Come on," she called. "The air is fine up here!"

Brevan slowly spread his arms. For a moment, he stood, looking up, then he began to rise vertically to her height. There, he leveled off, reclined at an angle, and executed a perfect rolling loop. He laughed delightedly. "How did I do that?"

For a while, they played, exploring the drafts and cross currents, learning to gauge their speed and direction. Sometimes the air narrowed without warning to a knife edge; sometimes, it fanned out, then faded. Here, it shot up sheer as through a chimney shaft; there, it plunged to the ground. They floated, they twisted, they dove; in arcs, circles, and straight lines.

Mylanfyndra missed a draft, tumbled head over heels toward the ground and landed with a jarring thud. She felt tired suddenly, which surprised her, considering how effortlessly she had ridden the winds.

Brevan landed with a hop and skip beside her. "How are you?"

"Shaky, now I'm down. But I'll be ready for more by tomorrow night."

"Tomorrow night? Can we come back so soon, Myl?"

Mylanfyndra grinned. "Can we *not?*" She went to where they had hidden the treasures. "Let's take a peep before we go."

They removed the seal and lifted out the bag. Mylanfyndra took up the collar, held it to her neck. "Help me put it on, Brevan."

"All right." Brevan slipped the collar around her neck and clicked the throat clasp shut. Again, the coldness, even in the summer's heat. Mylanfyndra cupped her hand over it, to speed its warming. Cold passed into her palm, warmth from her hand flowed into the collar: a fair exchange, she thought. "I wish we could know whose it was." She looked up. "If Gven did find it when he found us—do you suppose we're connected?"

"Wouldn't Gven have told us?"

"Maybe he was waiting until we were older."

"That sounds poss—" Brevan was staring at her throat. "Myl—the stone's lighted up again!"

She took off the collar, but even as she examined the stone, its glow faded, and it was dark and opaque as before. "My warmth must have awakened it. Now that it's cold again, it's gone back to sleep."

"You and your fancies, Myl." Brevan held out his hand. "Time to go."

"Oh, all right." Mylanfyndra handed over the collar reluctantly. "But from now on, I wear it while we're here."

The air grew hotter with each passing day. Demand for water increased; geth worked overtime hauling around the public water carts, refilling house cisterns from the town wells. In spite of the heat and their exhaustion, the children stole into the podlithra as often as they could, rising with the currents, mastering the airs. Floating high beneath the stars, Mylanfyndra thought wistfully of the sleeping fire-birds nestled in hollow podlith boles below. Oh, to see them once during the day! Now sleek gray bodies with wings of flame, they would be taking their first tentative flights, fluttering up toward the sun in dribs and drabs, beating the air above the twisted vine-tops with increasing strength . . .

As blue sky heated to gold, the birds circled for longer in ever-growing clusters, making ready to form one loud, piping **V** and fly away to join all the other birds in their secret refuge on the mesa.

In the town, folk watched the skies for the day when the many firebird flocks converged. For three days after, the single flock would circle the town, filling the air with urgent calls. On the third and final day, they would spiral up toward the sun, then head for the place that Gven had sought and never found. But by this time, no one watched to track where they went, for on that day, the Elders declared it time to evacuate into the Warren. On that day, the eve of the glair, spidery lines of violet light flickered in a sky turned copper, and blue fires flashed—sparks from Anlahr's approaching heels. Every year, despite the firebirds' timely warning, there was last-minute panic, but come the first storm, everyone was safely in the Warren.

For regular townsfolk, the Evacuation was a nuisance, but not so bad, for they could take as much as they wished to provide for thirty long days underground. Even Gven, who every year envied the awkward, flightless firebirds, wishing he could simply sprout wings and flee the glair as they did, had endured no real hardship, carrying to the Warren all the creature comforts that the broom cart could bear.

For geth, it was another matter.

One evening, Krels banged the pot. "The firebird flocks joined up today, in case you didn't hear their cries. Three days, folk," he announced. "Three days to the glair. You know the rules: one *small* roll each for the Warren. You had better start picking what to take."

Through the general murmur came grumbles and oaths.

If a firestorm hit the brug, as had happened eight times in the past twelve years, things left behind would flash to ash.

"Don't look so worried," Ebbwe said. "You've hardly anything. You can easily take all you've got. In fact, you'd better watch out that folks don't try to make you carry loads of their stuff for them."

Mylanfyndra said nothing. Only three more days, then no more rising for thirty more! How to survive so long without the freedom of the airs?

Three days dwindled to two. "Our last night tomorrow," Mylanfyndra declared, as they sat on the hilltop that night. "Oh, Brevan, how shall we stand it?" She looked around the ring of podliths, fixing every detail in her mind. "Tomorrow," she said suddenly, "let's dress up in our good clothes for Grandpa, since we shan't be seeing him for a while."

"Oh, Myl." Brevan smiled. "As if he'd care. But it's time for a change, anyway, the state these old things are in now."

Back in the brug, as they lay down to sleep, Mylanfyndra sat up again. "Did you hear?" She peered cautiously around their little island. Ebbwe was sleeping on her back, hand cushioning her cheek. Beyond, Fos lay curled tightly. The nearby families were all still, locked into the darkest hour of the morning. Mylanfyndra relaxed as, way down the hall, someone stirred and called out in a dreaming.

The next night, when all was still and dark, the children put on their best clothes and stole from the brug. The air was heavy, charged, even at that late hour, filling

Mylanfyndra with urgency. The last time they would creep through the town. The last time they would climb up through the podlithra. The last time they would visit Grandpa's knoll. The last time they would ride the airs for such a great long spell! By the time they reached the crest, Mylanfyndra couldn't wait to rise.

"What about your collar?" Brevan said.

"Later!" Mylanfyndra cried, and together they soared, higher than they had ever risen before. They played tag with the winds, then, spent, they drifted peacefully. Mylanfyndra gazed at the stars, the wind's hot breath wafting across her skin. Up here she was right and good. No one to look down on her, to watch that she didn't steal or cheat on her task. No one to shrink from touching her, to look upon her as trash. How fine, she thought, to feel this good always, and to have worthy work as in Gven's time. She touched her bare throat. "I'll just fetch the collar, Brevan."

"I'll come with you."

They descended briskly, but as they made for the treasure trove, a voice rang out and shadows sprang.

"In the name of the law: seize them!"

Toova!

CHAPTER 15

 They stumbled in silence through the dark streets, a mass of guards around them. Not taking any chances, Toova had linked the children together with heavy chains, the end of which she held firmly in her strong fist. Going down the slopes was bad enough, for Toova and the men kept getting snarled up in the tangle. But when they reached the flat, open ground, Toova set a savage pace, towing the children along, into the town, through the cobbled streets so fast they had to trot to keep up. No one spoke, not Toova, not the guards. The only sound was of breath coming short and hard from all sides. As they mounted the Moot steps, Brevan tripped, jarring Mylanfyndra's neck as his end of the chain pulled down.

"On your feet!" Toova snapped.

Brevan came up without a word and went on.

Not once had he looked her way, Mylanfyndra noticed. As they passed under the entrance arches, she threw him a covert glance and her spirit quailed. Brevan was terrified. And furious—with her. Mylanfyndra couldn't bear it, but she dared not say a word for fear of bringing down a tirade about her head. Oh, where were they going, and what was to happen? she wondered. If only someone would *speak!*

Toova drew them through the lobby, then up and down hallways, coming at last to massive double doors. Beyond them was the Moot Chamber, where weighty judgments and laws were passed. The spectators gallery was empty, it being the middle of the night, yet at the far end the seven Elders were all convened, on a dais behind a high bench. As Mylanfyndra neared, she recognized Daven-Elder second from the left; the rest she did not know.

Wess, looking undefinably disheveled in his brown livery, rapped a spike-tipped mace three times on the floor then called out their names.

"Brev-geth!"

"Myl-geth!"

So ugly, she thought. Folk thought them ugly now.

"Stand out," Wess said.

Bound by their chains, they moved forward awkwardly.

"Farther," Wess rapped. "Up to the bench."

The middle Elder spoke. "These are the accused?"

"Indeed, Prime-Elder." Toova, stepping from behind.

"Speak the charge," Prime-Elder said mildly.

Wess cleared his throat. "The charge is that these geth did this night commit foul and wicked act by means of agent or agents unknown."

"Specifically?"

"If it please your worships," Toova explained, "they did rise from the ground and move in the air as only the spirits should."

"Rise from the ground? That is a very serious charge," Prime-Elder said. "In fact, wellnigh unbelievable. You saw it yourself, Toova'ven-tuil?"

"Indeed I did."

"Give your account. And say how you witnessed it in the first place."

Toova coughed. "It came to my ears that certain geth were leaving the brug during the dark hours. I therefore kept watch for them this night."

"Ummm. Go on."

"Just past midnight, the two accused emerged through a hole in the rear wall of the brug and left their lawful area."

Daven-Elder raised a hand. "You did not stop them? Why not?"

Toova smoothed down her skirts. "So please your worship, I believe they removed Gven'bahr-brum prior to his Sending, and stole his belongings. I let them go, thinking they might lead me to the hiding place. Lucky I did," she went on, "or we would not have discovered their evil practice."

"Rising into the air, so you say? Describe it."

"They climbed to the top of a hill, then they performed some kind of ritual—spreading their arms and turning about. Whereupon, they shot into the air and rode the winds like—may the spirits pardon me—*Koos and Anlahr!*"

The Elders began talking together, all at once.

". . . fallen to some cursed influence . . ."

". . . inexplicable evil . . ."

Prime-Elder rapped for order. "Daven-Elder, you wish to be heard?"

"Indeed. I have spoken with these geth. They are not evil. Misguided, yes. Ill-reared. But capable of mending their ways."

Daven-Elder's neighbor spoke up. "With respect, Daven-Elder, this is not a mere question of *mending ways*. Those two are possessed. Their evil could infect us all."

"There is wisdom there," Prime-Elder said. "I say we must examine why such evil comes to threaten us. You, boy," he peered down at Brevan. "Explain what you're about."

Brevan remained silent.

Prime-Elder shifted his gaze to Mylanfyndra. "You, then. Tell us how and why you do this terrible thing. Speak, your lives may depend on it."

"It's not terrible," Mylanfyndra protested. "We do it because it comes to us like—like breathing. It feels natural and right."

More exclamations from behind the bench, and much shaking of heads.

Prime-Elder rapped for order. "Well we are agreed that what you do is not natural and not right. In fact, it is evil."

"No!"

"Perhaps," another Elder said, "the girl would tell us how long this has been going on?"

"Well," said Mylanfyndra, "it began shortly after—" She

broke off. Best not mention Grandpa. "Shortly after we moved to the brug. We felt so shut in, you see, after growing up in the podlithra. We began to feel strange in here." She tapped her chest bone.

"Indeed. How, strange?"

"As though we'd burst if we didn't have space to rise," Mylanfyndra said. "Like—oh, when you were young, didn't you ever want to run and run forever without stopping?"

The Elders stared down stiff-faced. As though, Mylanfyndra thought with a sinking feeling, as though she were a 'lithworm. Couldn't they understand what she was trying to say?

Prime-Elder was conferring once again with his fellows. Finally he turned to face the children. "It is of our opinion that you are showing symptoms of some terrible malady, an evil that you have somehow brought upon yourselves. Have you anything to say on that?"

Mylanfyndra felt the quick jerk of Brevan's head pulling on the chain. She remembered the first night of their rising, Brevan's misgivings.

Maybe it's a kind of ailment, Myl.

"With your permission, your worships." Toova spoke up. "I would remind you of how Gven'bahr-brum's body vanished prior to his Sending."

"Ah." Prime-Elder nodded. "So?"

"How and why—we may never arrive at the truth. Yet the fact remains Gven'bahr-brum did not have his Sending, and it is evident that the wyrth are now angry. Believing that we withhold body and gifts on purpose, they seek to punish us. So they curse these geth with this evil sickness.

Think, your worships, think what will happen when the sickness spreads and we all begin to rise in like fashion! Why, when Anlahr learns we make mockery of his power, he'll likely blow us to ash in a breath!"

"But why these geth?" Daven-Elder demanded, against the general murmur.

"They were the ones who removed Gven's body and stole his things. This, the wyrth must know, as they know all."

Daven-Elder surveyed the children over the table. "Did you do this? Did you remove Gven'bahr-brum's body from the hut and hide it somewhere?"

Mylanfyndra saw with a shock that Brevan had gone quite pale. All this talk of wyrth and evil sickness—he's of the same mind! Why, in another minute, he'll be telling everything! "No!" she cried.

"A lie, Daven-Elder," Toova said implacably. "Of course they'll lie to cover up their ill deeds and try to save themselves."

"Toova'ven-tuil," Prime-Elder said. "We commend your dedication in pursuing these geth, and your courage in apprehending them while knowing full well the risk of contamination. Evil they are, we cannot harbor them. They are as the creeping stone-blight on the podlithra: one tainted limb can fell the whole. They are as 'lith rats nesting in a house. If the nest be not destroyed, the whole house is razed."

Destroyed? Mylanfyndra stared, stunned, as the Elders conferred, leaning their heads together over the table top.

"We are not evil!" she yelled. "I say again that what we did felt good and right! Tell them, Brevan! Tell them how it really was!"

Brevan kept his head down, avoiding her eyes. As for the Elders, she might well not have spoken.

At last, Prime-Elder looked up, fixing his gaze on Toova. "We are now agreed upon this most solemn matter," he said. "Our judgment is this: that these geth not contaminate the people of our town, they shall straightway be taken to the market place and confined in the thieves cage. Tomorrow, come the Evacuation, we shall leave them to great Anlahr's judgment."

"All your fault." Brevan's accusation came quietly through the dark.

Mylanfyndra looked to the shadowy bulk huddled in the far corner of the cage, as far from her as possible. "Yes." She hung her head.

"We never should have left the brug. I was against it right from the beginning. But you would go meddling in what we do not understand!"

"We didn't meddle! It came from in here." She tapped her chest. "Those strange feelings, they grew on us, like firebirds' wings." At the very mention of the feelings, her chest tightened. She needed to fly, *now*. To rise up and flee this wretched place. And here she was, shut like vermin in a trap! Enraged, she banged her fist against the bars, startling the quiet. Quick as her anger came, it vanished, leaving only guilt. Her fault Gven had gotten sick. Her fault that they had kept him from the Sending. Her fault that they had left the brug. Her fault they had gone again and again into the podlithra to rise with the airs. "Do you really think we did wrong? Do you think us sick and possessed with evil?" she asked in a low voice.

"Yes. No. It makes no difference in the end."

The end.

Only Gven had witnessed a firestorm and lived. No one knew how many firestorms raged across the mesa; but Mylanfyndra had seen the aftermath: blackened stone, piles of ash. Ancient podliths split and shattered. Roof tile burned off the housetops. Metal pipe and cistern twisted, or melted into pocked and cindery lumps. Mylanfyndra wiped her forehead. The air was so heavy: thick as stip . . . Come dawn, folk would pass through the marketplace on route for the Warren, ordered to go out of their way to view the evil ones in the cage, so Toova said.

Mylanfyndra turned, pressing her back into the cage bars. Would the fire hurt? Or would it strike so fast they wouldn't feel it? The marketplace, cleared of booths, seemed to her like a giant oven . . .

"Sorry," she murmured. Brevan stood to face her.

"Me, too."

"What shall we do?"

"What *can* we do, Myl?"

They ran to the middle of the cage, and clung, comforting each other.

Dawn came, swift and merciless. Heat rushed up from the cobbles, stiffing the hairs on Mylanfyndra's arms. "I can't breathe," she said. "And I'm so parched already."

From overhead came the loud flap of wings. The firebirds had risen from their night roost in the podlithra and were swooping over the town, calling urgently. Their last day: they would go any time now. Mylanfyndra craned up through the cage bars. Thick as smoke they wheeled above the housetops, wings flared, crying freedom.

Toova appeared, with bread and water. "Even the evil don't go thirsty," she said, shoving it between the cage bars.

"You're the evil one," Mylanfyndra retorted. "Condemning us unfairly!"

The first people were coming past, eyeing the cage with caution.

"For shame." Toova raised her voice to the passersby. "Did you or did you not rise?"

"Yes," Brevan said, coming to Mylanfyndra's side. "But we—"

"Did you hear that?" Toova cried. "They admit their guilt barefaced!"

The square was filling now with folk toting bags and pushing carts. "For shame!" A man took up Toova's cry, setting off a chorus of jeers, drowning the firebirds' calls.

Mylanfyndra moved to the other side of the cage and turned her back on the crowd, peering up. At that moment, the wheeling flock scattered, then reformed into a long, ragged V and spiraled like a funnel up toward the molten sun. Behind her, Toova called for order, pointing.

"Good people, the sky darkens over the podlithra: the first storm is almost on us! We must move along with all speed!" she cried, and rushed away.

Mylanfyndra gazed over the clay roofs toward their old home. Sure enough, in that direction the brilliant sky was changing to coppery red.

The crowds hurried past, glancing their way. Widow

Mayfy appeared. "To think I had them in my house," she declared. "Before they were cursed," she added hastily. The laundry women went by in a gaggle, pointing, not one kind face among them.

"Take no notice," Mylanfyndra told Brevan. "Pretend they're not there."

"How can I? They're all around, treating us like vermin."

"Like geth," Mylanfyndra corrected. "Brevan—hold your head up. We're *not* sick. We're *not* evil, I don't care what they say!"

Toward noon, the red light deepened, casting a blood glow over the square, the cage bars, staining their flesh. It was so hot, the air, so heavy. Mylanfyndra felt as though giant arms were squeezing her ribs. The crowds thinned to a straggle. Krels came by, leading the geth. "Hey—you two! You going to tell me where you put Gven's things?" he said as he went past. "You won't need them now."

Mylanfyndra turned her back.

"Brevan! Myl!" Ebbwe, bringing up the rear. "The things they're saying, you wouldn't believe."

The children crouched and took her outstretched hands in silence.

"It was Vel," Ebbwe went on. "Toova paid her a whole grat. She's showing it to everyone, and Krels daren't touch it. I'll get her back, I—"

"Hey—you!" Krels was starting toward her.

Ebbwe pressed her face to the bars. "Don't give up—*all right?*" She ran, crashed into Krels, who rushed her on to vanish around the corner.

Don't give up? Mylanfyndra gazed around the empty square.

Brevan knelt beside the cage door, trying vainly to reach the bolt. But this was a thieves cage. Whoever had designed it had wisely set the catch below the floor. "If only," he said, gritting his teeth. He lay full length, tried again. Scrambling up, he tested the cage bars, tugging on each one in turn. Solid, all around the cage.

The light shifted ominously. Now a strange, luminous green tinge was washing through the copper. A flicker of violet light came from behind the podlithra. As they gazed up, a puff of hot wind blew through the cage.

Mylanfyndra shivered. "It's coming from over our way. It's the firestorm, isn't it?"

"I'm afraid so," Brevan said.

CHAPTER 16

A loud crack fractured the hush. Somewhere up in the podlithra, Anlahr's fire had struck.

"Back from the bars, Myl."

They huddled side by side in the middle of the cage, holding each other. Another, louder crack, sharp as a whip. "Oh!" Mylanfyndra hid her face.

"It's all right," Brevan said. "It won't hit us."

Mylanfyndra clung. "How can you know that!"

Rapid flashes lit the square, Mylanfyndra caught their brilliance, even though her eyes were covered. "All right for them," she muttered. "Safe in the Warren."

At a sudden shout, Mylanfyndra looked up. A small figure burst into the marketplace and raced toward them, waving.

"Ebbwe!" The children ran to the cage door.

Another crack. Ebbwe squealed, faltered, came on again.

"Here, Ebbwe! Under the floor! See the bolt? Back, pull it back!"

Ebbwe ducked out of sight. There was a snick and a scrape, then she popped up again, puffed and shiny. "There! Didn't I say don't give up?"

"Oh, Ebbwe, thank you!" Mylanfyndra raised the cage door with Brevan and jumped down. The Warren was not far, but even so. "That was quick."

"And easy. I hid till they'd all gone," Ebbwe boasted. "Then I sneaked out and—here I am. Here: food and water for a day or two, at least." From her pockets, she produced a pack and a battered flask and handed them to Mylanfyndra and Brevan respectively. "Stole them off a cart—don't worry," she added with a grin, as the children stowed the gifts inside their pockets. "Those folk had enough to last a whole year." She glanced up. "Hey, the sky's got green streaks now! *Aagh!*" she yelled as another crack split the air. "Have to go, good-bye."

"Wait—look the other way!" Brevan pointed back toward the podlithra. High in the sky, a fiery pillar whirled, advancing rapidly.

"Anlahr," Ebbwe whispered. "See the lightning shooting from his heels?" Jagged streaks, knife-edged, slashing the sky. "He's coming for us."

"For *us*. Go, Ebbwe. Go!" Mylanfyndra urged.

"Too late! He saw me let you out!" Ebbwe began to run. Rising winds cut through, flapping her skirts.

"Wait, Ebbwe." Mylanfyndra grabbed her arm and turned to Brevan. "She'll never make it on foot. We must carry her."

"*Carry* me?"

Mylanfyndra looked into Ebbwe's face. "They were partly right about us. We can ride the airs. Will you trust us?"

"But—it's gotten so wild up there," Brevan protested.

"We haven't far to go," Mylanfyndra argued. "If we move now, we'll outride that thing." She went behind Ebbwe and clasped the girl around the middle. "Ready?" she said. Mylanfyndra shot into the air—only to fall back a way, from the unexpected pull of Ebbwe's weight.

"Oooooh!" Ebbwe began to struggle. "Let me down!"

"Hold still!" Mylanfyndra cried, bobbing wildly with the force of Ebbwe's movements. "I've got you safe. Brevan, come *on!*"

Brevan rose unhappily. "I still don't like it, Myl. Those winds up there—we've experienced nothing like them. We'll have no control."

"We won't go that high," Mylanfyndra argued. They cast about, seeking a cliffward draft. A gust seized them and hurtled them high over the housetops.

"Ow!" Ebbwe squealed, then cried out delightedly. "Oh, look! You can see clear across town!" The current sheered, dipping them sharply. "Oh! Oh, I'm falling!" she shouted. "I'm going to be killed!"

"No, you're not. Close your eyes and keep still. You're hurting my arms!" Mylanfyndra shouted, as they bucketed about. She cast around, seeking the right draft. Easier to find a slip of broomstraw after the glair!

"Myl! This way!" Brevan beckoned. Mylanfyndra moved to his side and they rode the wild gusts on toward the Warren. They cleared the town, crossed a narrow belt of wasteland, and the Warren's low ridge loomed. Beyond it the Chute reared skeletal, the slide vanishing into thick mistwall.

At the sight of that wall, Mylanfyndra's blood thudded in her chest.

. . . it is evident that the wyrth are now angry . . .

But why these geth?

They removed Gven's body . . . the wyrth must know, as they know all . . .

Ebbwe screamed. "Look out! The wyrth!"

Brevan shouted. "Behind, Myl—behind!"

The fiery funnel was over the wasteland now.

Mylanfyndra gripped Ebbwe tighter, and kicked with all her might toward the Chute, alighting by the steps before Ebbwe knew it. There, she released Ebbwe, hugging her hard. "Good-bye—we'll never forget you!" she called, as the girl dashed for the low cave entrance.

Brevan hovered anxiously, his eye on the wyrth. Truly, it looked live, thrashing in the crosswinds; live, and menacing.

"Which way?" Mylanfyndra shouted. On one hand, the

wyrthwall. On the other, the fire pillar was now so near she could hear it spit and spark.

"Let's circle around it." Brevan waved his arm in a wide arc back across town toward their former home. Mylanfyndra nodded. They should be safe in the firestorm's wake.

Side by side, they detoured around the flaming whirl-wind, over the town, toward the podlithra. Mylanfyndra glanced down at the Moot Hall's mass. "Brevan, we could shelter down there."

Brevan shook his head. "We'd never reach it. And they've surely sealed the doors!"

Mylanfyndra looked back. "Brevan!" The fire column had turned about as they had, and was overtaking along their path. "Anlahr pursues us! I'm going down!" She made to dive, but giant winds lifted her as if she were an ash plume. Hot dry gusts clapped against her eardrums, and the sky darkened even further. Brevan's shape wavered, merging with the murk. "Brevan—help!"

"Here—take my hand!" Brevan grabbed her and hung on as together they were swept from the town and up into the podlithra. Mylanfyndra's head cleared, but the sky re-mained dark. Was it night? Or the storm's aftermath?

"Myl!" She looked down. Below them, Gven's hut—in flames!

A sudden blast tumbled them high into the air. Mylan-fyndra's hand was torn from Brevan's grasp, her breath snatched from her lungs. One moment, she hung, weight-less. The next, in a rush of air, she was falling, fast.

Mylanfyndra opened her eyes. She was lying on doft—

124

under a black sky. "What am I—" she began, then it all came rushing back; the cage, Ebbwe, the firestorm. And falling. Was the storm over? She sat up. No sign of fire pillar. Not much wind now, either. She sniffed, smelled smoldering vine.

She got to her feet, wincing. "Brevan?" He couldn't be far. She called again. Was he hurt? She limped painfully for a few feet, then stopped to rub her ankle. Why bother walking? She would rise and find the Grandpa Grove. Brevan would likely be waiting for her there. She cleared the podlith tops cautiously, then, finding the air still calm, rose higher, circling until at last she spied Grandpa's knoll.

Empty. Mylanfyndra alit beside Gven's grave. "A fine mess, Grandpa," she muttered. "They put us out to die in the firestorm. We managed to escape, but now I've lost Brevan." She licked her lips, found them dry and bitter-tasting. Mylanfyndra patted her pocket. She had the food; Brevan carried the water. "I need a drink, Grandpa. I won't be long."

Mylanfyndra descended on foot. The doft was warm, even hot in places, she found, picking her way down the slope. Of the hut, only the smoking walls remained. The cistern was a twisted metal heap, too hot to touch. She cupped her hands to her mouth and shouted.

"Brevan! Brevan!"

There was no reply.

She climbed back to the hilltop, shouting his name hoarsely all the way. "He won't answer, Grandpa," she croaked. "He must be hurt." Or asleep. Unless . . . he had been swept on by those ferocious winds. Swept where? She paced the clearing anxiously, then, on a thought, she fetched out the treasure bag, put the collar on, and at once felt comforted. She made to replace the bag, changed her mind, and hung it on her belt. "I'm so worried, Grandpa," she announced. "I'm going to scout for Brevan. I know I can't see, but I can call his name." Yes, a good idea. "If he comes, tell him to wait: I'll be back."

Mylanfyndra rose a few feet, then hovered. Where to start? Over the podlithra, she supposed, for that was where they had been torn asunder. She began to sweep out from the hilltop in circles, calling her brother's name.

Suddenly, wind sprang up, buffeting her body. Then it caught her, swept her higher. A red glow crept from behind the podlithra. Dawn? Or another firestorm? Silent lightning flickered. A storm, and she out in the open!

"Brevan! Brev—*a-a-a-a-an!*"

Oh, where was he! Mylanfyndra skimmed the podliths urgently. Another flash. Following the same path as before, the noisy winds swept her down from the podlithra and on toward the town.

Would another fire pillar come? Mylanfyndra fought furiously to stay where she was, thinking of Brevan lying exposed to Anlahr's fury. But she was no match for those prevailing currents. Relentlessly, they hurtled her across the town, and over the wasteland toward the Warren.

The wyrthwall seethed, mist fingers writhed, curling to reach her. Mylanfyndra braced herself, while remembering how last time the wind had looped back on itself at the very brink. Turn about, she urged the wind. Turn *now!*

But this time it swept her past the Warren, off the cliff, and out into the mist.

PART SECOND

CHAPTER 17

Mylanfyndra waited, rigid, for Anlahr's fury to engulf her. The wind cut, and all was hushed and still. Out here, no dull red glow of firestorm, only darkness. But all around, she could feel mist; fine, cool spray that soothed her hot, dry skin. She let go, some, and touched the golden collar. Had it protected her? "Did you bring me luck after all?" she said aloud. "If so, don't forget Brevan: he's the one who saved you first. Help me find him—please?"

Almost at once, the air lightened. The night was over, another day had begun. She peered into the pearling mist, uneasy again. Drifting over the wyrth domain . . . She must get back onto the mesa—but which way?

A light draft stroked her face. A sign? Mylanfyndra followed it a way, but the mist went on. Surely the mesa was not that distant? She pulled back then struck out again going all ways, though not too far in any one direction until—"Ah!"

The mesa at last!

Breaking through under a golden sky, Mylanfyndra scanned the mesa cliffs. Odd: no Warren, no Chute. And . . . the gray of the doft was broken by large red patches. She had never seen red clay on the mesa; only the blue-gray of doft and podlith. Gven, who had walked the cliffs around, had never mentioned such. So where was she, then? She flew on along the cliff edge, one hour, two, finding nothing but the piebald clay. Spying a cluster of loose rocks, Mylanfyndra alighted, frowning. In among the gray boulders reared red ones, high above her head. "Strange," she murmured. "Red clay. Now tall red rock. What can have happened?"

She sat, leaning up against the rock. Above her, the white-hot sun blazed down, scarcely discernible in the brilliant sky. She wiped her forehead. Her belly was empty and her mouth, dry. She pulled out Ebbwe's food pack, unwrapped it, and found hard biscuit and a bundle of sweet root. She nibbled some biscuit, pulled a stick of root to suck, then firmly stowed the rest. No knowing how long it had to last, she told herself uneasily.

Time was wasting. Still chewing on the root, Mylanfyndra rose, and moved on around the mesa's edge. For hours, she flew, watching for the familiar landmark of town or Warren, until, at last, she spied a cluster of rocks at the cliff edge. She sped toward it, then halted, hovering over it in confusion. It was the same cluster that she had seen before! "I've come full circle!" she cried. So where was the Warren? And the town? "Doesn't make sense," she muttered, "unless—" *Unless this was another mesa entirely. . . .* Impossible!

Or was it? Could there be another mesa? Mylanfyndra gazed over the strange red-and-gray ground. Had to be! Another mesa besides theirs, and no one ever dreaming it! But now she must get back to hers, and Brevan.

Mylanfyndra soared above the mist to take her bearings, but found the brilliance blinding. She retreated back down into the shelter of the haze. Which way? She touched the throat clasp. "You're my lucky stone. Help me," she whispered. Wind puffed against her face, swirling the mist. Was this another sign? Should she follow its drift? As if in answer, the wind strengthened, nudging her along. She had not gone far off her mesa, so any time now, Mylanfyndra told herself hopefully, she must break out back over the Warren. But the wind, gathering force and purpose, only bore her forward through mist that stretched on and on. The sun went down, the sky went dark.

Thirsty, Mylanfyndra pulled another root stick and sucked its sappy juice. Then sometime after that, she simply closed her eyes and drifted. . . .

She came to, and realized that she must have fallen asleep. Asleep—while riding the winds? For how long? It was still dark, though way to her right, the mist was lightening into coppery red. Dawn, or a coming storm? Mylanfyndra rose up high, cleared the mist to look—and caught her breath in shock. Mesas, more than she could count—and all of them red! Not a gray one in sight, the round, red plateaux

spread away like giant paving stones, mist-embedded, clear to the horizon! She covered her face. Lost—utterly lost!

Mylanfyndra turned and turned about, then resolved to move on. But which way? The current that had carried her from the red-and-gray mesa still blew, like a sky road, in one steady direction. Should she turn about and fly back up that road, retracing her path; or follow it forward? "If the wind brought me this way, then it likely brought Brevan, too. So I should follow it," she reasoned. She pressed on, over bare red mesas scorched by Anlahr's breath and wrapped in walls of mist.

As the day passed, Mylanfyndra grew hungry and very thirsty. Mesa after barren mesa: no people, no wells. She bit on biscuit, which made her more thirsty then ever, and chewed more root, sucking on the sap. The sun passed overhead, then climbed down. Dazed, exhausted, she went in and out of sleep.

"Surely, this cannot go on much longer," she told herself. "The world cannot be much bigger than this."

Night fell, and Mylanfyndra was moving on through darkness. When dawn came, she was still moving, riding the windcurrent. Too late to turn back, she knew it now. Fighting panic, she kicked forward, resolving to move ahead with all the speed that she could muster. Around noon, the biscuits were all gone, and one root stick remained.

Below, the dry red mesas stretched to the horizon, seemingly forever.

"Water," she muttered, "I'm so thirsty, I must find water soon!"

Now the wind changed, sweeping her strongly to the left. In a daze, Mylanfyndra suffered it to bear her along, while the sun climbed down in the sky. Suddenly, she noticed with a start that the sunset was clear and radiant, the sort that came in Anlahr's wake. "Can't be," she said. "The glair has only just begun."

Intrigued, Mylanfyndra flew faster, while the sun slid out of sight and a half-moon floated up in a luminous blue-green wash, star-sprinkled. All at once, a dark, unbroken line of cloud loomed on the horizon—no! Not cloud, but solid cliffs, cliffs so high that they outsoared their mistwall. As she reached them, she saw that flaming torches marked the cliff edge. People! She dove a way, then pulled up, rising higher. What if they were not friendly?

Back from the cliffs was a square building with tall chimneys from which came a familiar, rotten smell. Men toiled from cliff to building with cartloads of yellow dust that seemed to glow in the twilight. Ladders hung from the cliff, down into the mist. Men climbed them, baskets of the yellow stuff on their backs. Beyond, two men turned a capstan, winching up a thick rope that dangled into the mist. A man was leaning over, looking down. "Get a move on," he shouted. "It's my suppertime!" He gave the rope a sharp tug.

From below, there came a cry of pain, and a small figure shot up into the clear: Brevan!

Brevan, a noose around his neck, a basket of the yellow stuff strapped to his back. They hauled him onto the clifftop, unhitched the basket, tipped its contents into a waiting wagon. Freed of his load, Brevan sank to his knees, while the foreman unhooked him from the rope and put him on a leash.

"I'm off to lock him up," the foreman told the winch crew, yanking Brevan back onto his feet. "You bring in the rest." He dragged Brevan toward the building.

Mylanfyndra dove, feet first. "Ouf!" The shock of hitting the man's wide back jarred the wind from her lungs. But the man went down, the leash flying from his hand, and the winch crew scattered.

"Rise, Brevan!" Mylanfyndra yelled.

Brevan rose, leash dangling, and they took off into the dark. "Myl! How did you find me?"

"Followed my nose," she called, catching a whiff of him. "You stink!"

"It's the charvis." Brevan tugged at his leash. "Get this off me?"

"Charvis?" Mylanfyndra closed in, untied the knots, and let the leash fall. "What's that?"

"The yellow powder. Thanks, Myl." Brevan rubbed his neck, wincing. Below, figures ran all over, shouting, pointing up into the dark.

"Wait here, will you? I'm going for food."

Going? "No—wait—don't leave me!" Mylanfyndra cried, but Brevan was gone toward the mass of clustered chimneys. She started to follow, then thought better of it. Brevan possibly knew his way around; she certainly did not. Mylanfyndra circled the chimneys anxiously, up one draft, down another, watching for her brother to reappear. Minutes passed. She was just beginning to worry, when a light tap on her shoulder made her cry out.

Brevan laughed. "See how crafty I am now?"

"Pity you weren't earlier, then they wouldn't have caught you," she retorted, angry and relieved at once.

"Hah! You're only jealous. Hey," Brevan said, taking her hand, "you're icy. Come on, we'll clear this place, then stop and eat." He held up a small package. "Bread and root pie—and some squishy fruit."

"*Squishy fruit?*"

"It's big and soft and full of juice—good as water, Myl."

"I'd rather not stop," she said, looking back toward the cliffs. Not here, where those men had caught Brevan.

"Oh, all right. We'll eat on the way. Here." Brevan handed her a chunk of bread.

"On the way where?" Mylanfyndra took the bread, bit hungrily into the crust, found that she could hardly chew it, her mouth was so dry.

Brevan pointed up. "See where that big star lies?"

"Which one?" The night sky all looked the same to Mylanfyndra.

"That blue one? Never mind. They call that way north. That's where people are. We'll head for there."

They skimmed moonlit plain. No sign of people—or of mist, either. "This mesa is huge," Mylanfyndra shouted across to Brevan. "There is no end to it."

"It's not a mesa; it's one huge, big land," Brevan called back. "Here: try some of this."

He pushed something soft and sticky into her hand. Mylanfyndra touched it warily to the tip of her tongue. "The squishy fruit?" It was sweeter, more succulent than anything she had ever tasted. She bit into it, felt the juice explode into her parched mouth. "Is there any more?"

" 'fraid not," Brevan called back. "But we'll find some place to eat by morning, you'll see."

They flew on in silence until, at last, the sky began to lighten. Below them, dull brown plain. No people. No food. No water.

"I thought you said there were people this way."

"The land is bigger than I realized. You're wearing the collar, Myl."

Mylanfyndra's hand went up. "For luck. I shan't take it off."

"Well, not yet," Brevan conceded. "Did you bring the other things?"

Mylanfyndra nodded, patting her apron.

To their right hand, the sun rose in a milky blue sky with drifting veils of thin white cloud. "Where's the glair?" Mylanfyndra said.

"There is none here, Myl."

"No glair?" Did Anlahr not come this way? Mylanfyndra was about to ask, when something bright winked on the horizon. "What's that?"

"Something metal, by the look of it. Let's go see." As they flew toward it, the gleam grew bigger and brighter. "It's a well—no, it can't be!" Mylanfyndra cried. It was much too large. Besides, there was no wall or pump house, just a plain hole in the ground filled with shining water. "And what are those?" Surrounding the water, tall, straight poles crowned by leaves that waved in the wind like great, green plumes!

They landed cautiously near the water's edge, on a mat of leaves and flowers. "This is a puzzle," Mylanfyndra said. "A pumpless well in the middle of nowhere, and all these green growing things around it." She knelt by the hole, and, cupping her hands, drank greedily. The water was cold, with a faint salt tang. She drank until she could drink no more, then she splashed her head and face. She would like to have jumped into the hole and bathed all over, but, as Gven had taught them, one didn't wash in water from which one must drink. She sat back on her heels with a sigh. "I'm starving, Brevan."

"Me, too." Brevan gazed all around, then up. "Myl— see there?" Where leaf met stem hung clusters of small, oval objects, like eggs. "It looks like squishy fruit."

They rose, and found that, indeed, it was. They plucked armfuls of the soft, green fruit and hurried down to eat it.

"Ummm." Brevan spat out a mouthful of seed. "We had stacks of these things in the camp. Aren't they sweet?"

Mylanfyndra could only nod. Brevan wandered around

the water's edge, pushing the sand with his toe. "Hey, what's this?" He knelt, and, scraping at the sand, pulled out a half-buried bowl. "What a lucky find. Now I can wash off this charvis stink."

Charvis again. "What is it?"

"A powder. You get it from the bottom of the cliffs." Brevan's face went stiff. "Oh, Myl. You'll never guess the terrible time I've had. When I landed on those cliffs, it was so dark that I never saw the ladders or the men. I lay down and fell asleep. When I awoke, I was locked up inside the refinery—that big building. Jag—he's the foreman—had seen me land and followed me. He put me to work with the charvis crews. It's terrible stuff to handle as I soon found out—see?" He held up his palm to display a patch of raw skin.

"Oh, Brevan. It looks like a burn."

"It *is* a burn. Charvis eats through to the bone if you don't catch it in time."

Mylanfyndra shuddered. "Why do they gather it?"

"Jag says their apothecaries use it for remedy."

"Some remedy that shreds off your skin!" Mylanfyndra cried.

"That's nothing. Men even die to get it." Brevan's face was stiff again. "Below the cliffs, mud boils in huge holes; scalding steam blows up from cracks in the floor." He turned on her. "That's the wyrth, Myl. There are no spirits—only steam."

"But the mist is cool, Brevan."

"Of course it is, by the time it gets all the way up here! But down there—" He scowled. "The noise is terrifying—

like a great kettle boiling over. You can hardly see, and you have to watch every step you take, to dodge the holes and cracks. Even if you're careful, the ground's so thin in places, it just caves in. I saw a man—" Brevan turned away abruptly.

Mylanfyndra put her arms around him. "Well, you're out of it now," she said. This place didn't sound any better than the mesa. She thought of the charvis crews left behind. "Those poor geth," she said.

"They aren't geth, Myl. There are no geth here. Those crewmen are thieves and killers from the north working off their crimes."

"And you were forced to work among them? What was Jag doing?"

Brevan shrugged. "Just using me. He saw I'd be quicker, not needing a ladder. The more charvis they bring up, the more he gets paid. But he'll catch it for using me, the others said so."

"What else did you learn about this place, Brevan?"

"Not much." Brevan picked up a squishy fruit, bit into it thoughtfully. "Only that they call where we come from the mesa belt. Its proper name is the Gansor, which means 'studded belt'."

"Gansor." Mylanfyndra repeated the name carefully. It sounded harsh and spare and unforgiving. "You didn't tell them we came from there?"

"Not exactly." Brevan laughed. "After they caught me, they all said that's where I'd come from. They meant it as a joke, Myl. Seems they think nobody lives off their cliffs."

"They're not the only ones," Mylanfyndra retorted. "But

they're almost right, Brevan. All those mesas I flew over I never saw another soul. Anyway, where are we now?"

"I have no idea." Brevan popped the last piece of fruit into his mouth, spat out the pips, and licked the juice off his fingers. "Tell you one thing, though. Jag wasn't exactly surprised at my flying," he said slowly. "In fact . . ." He threw her an odd look. "He said I wasn't *that* special."

Mylanfyndra sat up. "What else did he say?"

"Nothing. When I asked him some more, he got angry."

"Oh, Brevan. I wonder." Mylanfyndra pulled the pouch from under her apron and took out the medallion. "These people—could they be here, on this land?" Beautiful golden people who could ride the air!

Brevan frowned. "What makes you say that?"

"What you just said, about Jag taking you in his stride. Oh, Brevan, suppose one of these people dropped this pouch on our mesa—wouldn't they be glad to get it back? Oh!" She sat up.

"Now wait a minute," Brevan said. "You're running ahead too fast."

"No, I'm not." Mylanfyndra scrambled to her feet. "Haven't you thought? They fly, like us. What if—what if somehow we and they *belong!*" Excitedly, Mylanfyndra stowed the medallion, and restored the pouch to her belt. "Let's go," she said.

CHAPTER 18

Filling their pockets carefully with the pulpy fruit, they took their bearings by the sun, then pressed on north. The sun was sinking way to the left, when, ahead, they discerned low hills. Beyond the hills, a flat, round basin; in it, houses lay like dry, brown dregs.

Brevan started down.

"Wait." Mylanfyndra pulled him back. "Remember last time?"

"We must touch ground somewhere."

"But not here." The golden folk wouldn't live in that scrubby place. "Let's go. Listen," Mylanfyndra said, as Brevan balked, "if we don't find a better town within a day, we'll come back."

"It's getting dark," Brevan argued. "I need rest. And more to eat than fruit. Please, Myl," he pleaded, as

Mylanfyndra shook her head. "The folk can't all be like Jag. And we won't go down till after dark."

Mylanfyndra wavered. The smoke from the chimneys reminded her of home. "Maybe there's no harm. But remember," she warned, taking off the collar and stowing it, "we keep to ourselves and trust no one, agreed?"

The moonlit street curved through the town like a length of vine, with narrow, twisting alleyways leading off to either hand. They alit and stood, gazing down the street. Mylanfyndra trailed her fingers along the nearest house wall. Not build of podlith shards this, but brown clay scratched with patterns. And the houses: two-storied, with overhanging

gables! And she had thought the mesa houses grand! Instead of clay tile, the roofs wore thatch, and the windows were huge—why not, with no threat of firestorm? Farther down the street, people strolled, wrapped against the cool night.

Mylanfyndra shrank under a gable. "I don't like it."

"It's all right, I think. No one's looking our way."

Mylanfyndra stared, surprised. Brevan had surely grown bolder in the few days since the mesa, and now she was the wary one! She trailed him past a large building full of folk seated at tables loaded with food.

Brevan paused, sniffing. "Smells so good," he whispered. "Hey, Myl, look. They're buying that stuff. We could, too; we still have half-grats."

"Are you mad! Remember what we agreed, Brevan."

"Oh, come on. I'm starving."

Mylanfyndra hedged. "Let's look around first. I'll feel more easy."

"Oh, all right," Brevan said. "You'll only fuss until we do."

They went on, until, suddenly, the main street opened up on either side into a wide space, like the market square back home. They set out toward the street's continuation at the far side, until, all at once, Mylanfyndra halted.

Brevan turned back. "What's up, Myl?"

"Didn't you hear?" Footsteps behind. Now that she had stopped, they had stopped, also. She looked around. "We're so exposed out here, Brevan."

"Then let's go around by the edge."

"All right." She moved with Brevan to the edge of the square, then went on under the house gables as before. They were about halfway around, when, reaching the corner of a side alley, Mylanfyndra stopped once more.

"Someone is still behind us, Brevan." She took his arm. "Let's rise."

"Now you're the crazy one. We do that, if someone is there, they'll see us, and we'll have to leave and then we won't eat." Brevan glanced into the alley. "Let's duck down here. If someone does come after us, then we rise."

Mylanfyndra nodded doubtfully. "If you say so." They dodged into the alley and pressed themselves into the wall. A moment later, Mylanfyndra heard light footsteps, approaching rapidly. Then a figure burst out, blocking the alley entrance. A woman, massive, mantled shape dark against the moonlit cobbles; menacing. "Children?"

Mylanfyndra seized Brevan's hand, tugged his arm fiercely. *See?* the gesture said. "Rise—now!" she cried.

They shot up—and hit overhanging gables, gables so wide they almost touched across the alley, leaving no room to pass between!

"Ow!" They tumbled back onto the cobbles with a clatter.

"Children?" The woman was still there; no way could they run around that one. *What to do?*

Another voice came from the alley. "Here—you two: over here!" An old man, by the sound of it.

They looked to the woman's dark shape—like Toova's, Mylanfyndra thought, frightened.

As one, they ran down the alley. "That's right," the man urged. "Here, over to your left!" He beckoned from an open doorway, dimly lit. "Quick, inside," he said.

They hesitated, until, hearing the woman's footsteps approaching, they ran for the door. The moment they were through, the old man shut and bolted it. And there they stood, stone-still, in a tiny front hall, while the steps went past, fading down the alley. Mylanfyndra breathed out. That monstrous Toova-woman crowding the alley entrance! "Who was she?"

"Eh, I wouldn't know," the old man said. "There's more strangers than townsfolk in Ludder's End any day of the year."

"Ludder's End? Is that what you call this place?" Brevan said.

"Aye. It's the last outpost before you cross the charnon."

"Charnon?"

"Where are you two from?" The old man laughed, just like Gven. "The charnon's the desert from here to the Edge—the cliffs at the edge of the Gansor, if you didn't know that either. You're not headed there, I hope?"

"Oh, no," Brevan said.

Mylanfyndra moved to the door. "We're so grateful to you for hiding us. But now we must be on our way."

The old man smiled. "As you wish. But you're welcome to a bite of supper before you leave. While you're eating it, I could go see if that woman's really gone."

The children looked to each other uncertainly. "Supper?" Brevan said.

Mylanfyndra scrutinized the old man's face. His eyes were gray, like Gven's, and they seemed quite kindly. And he *had* just saved them from the Toova-woman. Even so. "I'm not sure," she began.

"That's kind of you," Brevan said. "We were about to have supper."

"Well, isn't that a lucky thing?" The old man led them into a tiny kitchen bright with firelight. "By the way, I'm Calen."

"I'm M-Mill," Mylanfyndra amended quickly. "This is my brother, Brev."

"Mill and Brev . . ." Calen cocked an eye toward them. "Well, Mill and Brev, you just make yourselves easy while I heat us some durrerry," he said, turning to the hearth.

Durrerry? The children eyed each other askance.

Calen produced a cooking pot, and, from an earthen bowl in the hearth, spooned out thick, black paste. Mylanfyndra made a face. That was durrerry?

"Lucky I was home tonight," Calen said over his shoulder. "Tomorrow, I'm off on my travels—I'm a goyar," he added.

Goyar. Another new word. Mylanfyndra would dearly like to know what a goyar was, and why he traveled, but dared not reveal their ignorance.

The room was filling with a sweet, spicy aroma. "Smells

146

good," Brevan said. "Actually, sir, I'm starving."

"Then eat," Calen said, and left.

They ate fast, were just finishing when Calen came back. "She's waiting at the corner, and looks set to stay. Sorry to say, this is a blind alley, and that's the only way out, so you'll not get away for a while." He poured them a hot, sweet drink smelling of some strange fragrance. Mylanfyndra took a tentative sip. All these new smells and flavors . . . delicious!

The old man watched them drink, looking quite concerned. "You could stay here the night," he offered, pointing to a low brown door beside the hearth. "I have room. It's only a humble hole in the wall, I'm afraid, but it's warm from the hearth. At least you'll be safe until morning."

"Well, perhaps," Brevan said. "It's very kind of you."

Calen opened the door and ushered them through.

It was warm in there, all right. Quite hot and stuffy, in fact. The tiny, windowless chamber was bare save for bulging sacks stacked against the walls, empty ones lying haphazardly about the tiles.

"Sorry there's no bed, but you'll find the sacks soft enough if you pile them up," Calen said, squeezing in behind them and closing the door.

As it swung to, Mylanfyndra cried out. Behind it was a large cage, waist-high. In it, a brown furry creature with tufted ears and a long tail bobbed up and down.

"What's *that?*"

"Brok, my dancing koury. Every goyar has one." He

tapped the bars, and the creature bared its sharp, white teeth in a frenzy of chatter.

Mylanfyndra eyed them uneasily. "Does it—bite?"

Calen laughed. "If you go too close." To Mylanfyndra's horror, he opened the cage door and stepped aside. Exclaiming shrilly, the creature leapt onto Calen's shoulder.

Mylanfyndra shrank back, glancing to the door. "Well," she said. "We're grateful for your kind offer, but we really ought to go."

"Go?" The old man smiled. "Oh, I don't think you'll be going anywhere for a while—at least, not without me. Ask your brother."

Mylanfyndra whipped around. "Brevan!"

He lay on the tiles, eyes closed. Mylanfyndra made to crouch beside him, but as she went down her head began to spin, and the tiny room went dark. She tried to steady herself, felt her knees give under her. As she sank down, Calen bent, said something in her ear, but she never heard a word.

CHAPTER 19

"Myl! Myl! Will you wake up!"

Mylanfyndra opened her eyes. Someone was whimpering. Not her, she realized thankfully. It was the koury, Brok, scratching at its cage bars. She sat up, found her feet shackled by heavy chains.

"What happened?" Brevan's feet were shackled also.

"Calen happened, what do you think?" he said bitterly.

Mylanfyndra recalled Calen's mocking face as she fell, his mouth forming words she couldn't hear. She kicked out in disgust, rattling the chains on the tiles. "He seemed so nice. Like—"

"Gven. I know."

"It's all because of that Toova-woman," Mylanfyndra said. "Who was she? What did she want? You don't suppose she saw us coming down, Brevan?"

"Maybe," Brevan said miserably. "But whether or no,

she's after us. Everywhere we go, someone's out to get us, seems like."

"Oh!" Mylanfyndra patted her apron. The pouch was still there, thank goodness. But best not to push their luck. "We must hide the treasure before Calen comes in."

"By all means," Brevan said sarcastically, looking around the bare room. "And where do you propose to do that?"

In one corner lay a heap of sacks, covered in dust and cobwebs. Mylanfyndra leaned over and slid the pouch under the pile—only just in time. The latch clicked, and Calen poked his head in.

"Ah," he said brightly. "I thought I heard you. You look better for a night's sleep—a good thing, for we're going out." He held up a mess of leather straps. "Harnesses. Can't have you getting ideas now, can I?"

"Ideas?" Mylanfyndra said.

Calen threw the harnesses down. "Get them on, quickly. You're going to make a pile of money for Uncle Calen before this day is through."

"How?" Mylanfyndra made no move toward the harnesses. "How can we possibly help you?"

"By rising, child. The folk will love it." He chuckled. "Goodness knows, they were taken enough with Brok, who can only hop and turn a somersault."

"Rising?" Brevan said.

Calen laughed. "Don't try to deny it. I saw you both in the alley last night. Up, my lucky children; let's have these things on."

Calen led them, shackled, and harnessed, to the front door. Outside, the alley was dim under the gables, even though the sun was out. Beside Calen's door was a fat red pole, capped by a big, brass knob.

"My goyar's sign," Calen said. "So folk know where to come for my services. Here, let's get you stowed." Calen hoisted them into a waiting handcart, bending up their knees, squashing them in side by side. Then he fastened down the cart cover, sealing them in.

The cart moved off up the alley, bumping painfully over the cobbles. Calen was going to make them rise in front of people? Mylanfyndra's face grew hot at the thought. "I wish we'd never stopped here," she whispered fiercely.

"It's my fault," Brevan said. "You warned me."

Mylanfyndra agreed silently, then repented. "And then I followed you. You didn't make me, so we're both to blame."

The cart paused briefly at the end of the alley, then turned left.

"Where are we going?" Mylanfyndra whispered.

"How should I know? To someplace where folk will pay to see us rising," Brevan answered miserably.

"I won't do it," Mylanfyndra cried. "I'd rather die."

"Me, too," Brevan declared loudly. "People who use people are wicked."

"I wouldn't say that," Calen said. "Your average goyar simply seeks the greatest good for the greatest number— of gold pieces, that is, haha! After tonight, we'll tour the frontier towns. Oh, my, in one season I'll be the richest goyar on Telfyra!"

"No chance," Brevan snapped. "When folk see that you're using us, they'll make you let us go."

Calen chuckled. "Don't count on it. Where we're going, folk don't ask, don't tell." The cart jolted on. Mylanfyndra's legs went numb. "It's so hot," she said. "There's no air in here. Brevan, I can't breathe!"

"Stop your whining," Calen said affably. "We're here." He halted the cart, lifted the cover, and air rushed in. Mylanfyndra sucked it in hungrily, then screwed up her face at the smell.

Calen bent down. "You lose the shackles, but keep the harnesses. See this?" He held up a bright red mace with a brass knob, a smaller version of the pole beside his door. "Look happy or you get this, understood?"

The children nodded.

Removing their chains, Calen set the children down onto a weedy sidewalk that shimmered with late morning heat. The moment Mylanfyndra touched ground, her legs buckled under her. She clung to the cart, chafing life back into her

153

limbs, hopping from one foot to the other as pins and needles started.

They stood outside a tavern with sagging roof and crumbling walls. From the open door odors of food, and ale, and flesh flowed out into the street. The goyar seized their reins and prodded them forward. "In you go—and remember what I said!" he warned, pushing them inside.

Folk looked up as they moved through the mess of noisy, crowded tables.

"What you got there, Calen?"

"Where's that beast of yourn? We want to see some tricks!"

"Hey—young 'uns aren't allowed in here!" A woman bustled forward, tying her apron.

"Ah, Leulah, don't be so fussed. These two are just about to make you a richer and happier woman."

"Away with you," the woman said, her eyes darting from Calen to the children and back again. "You and your smooth talk! Get them out of here."

"I do that and you'll be sorry," Calen said easily. "Here, give us an ale, then I'll show you what they can do." He sauntered on to a corner booth and sat, hauling in the children to squat at his feet.

Mylanfyndra looked up. Huge wheels crusted with clumps of halfspent tapers hung from the rafters. Above the rafters, the sun struggled in through grimy skylights. "We shan't rise," she muttered, staring defiantly at the dirty panes. "He can't make us."

"He'll beat us with that stick."

"That woman will stop him."

"Don't count on it," Brevan whispered. Mylanfyndra's heart contracted. Poor Brevan. She saw him back on the cliff, Jag hauling on his leash . . . Anger surged. "When I say *now,* we run for it," she whispered in his ear. But he didn't even turn his head. Had he heard?

Leulah banged a mug down before Calen, slopping warm ale onto the table top. "I'll see your money, goyar."

Calen hooked an arm through Brevan's reins, freeing his drinking hand. "Leulah, you shall."

"Now!" Mylanfyndra said.

They sprang.

Calen's hands shot out, and jerked the children back to sprawl under the table. Bending low, the goyar shook the brass knob in their faces. "Fools! Brok's ten times as quick!" he said, and rapped them on the shins.

Pain shot through Mylanfyndra's legs, she barely kept from crying out.

"Now," Calen said amicably. "For that, I hitch your harnesses to the back of my chair, see?" He looped Mylanfyndra's harness over one chair post, Brevan's over the other. The straps tightened, lifting them into a half-crouch, their heads pressed up against the underside of the table. "Now," he said, "stay quiet and good while I wet my whistle."

The children eyed each other hopelessly across Calen's knees. There was no way out, no way out at all.

Calen smacked the table with his mace and dragged the children up from under. "On your feet," he said. "I'm about to make my first pitch." He rapped again. "Good folks," he cried. "Pray silence."

The uproar faded to a buzz.

"Thanks, one and all. You are about to see a feat the like of which no one in Ludder's End has ever witnessed."

"Oh, yes?"

"We've heard that one before!"

"Tell us about it!"

The goyar smiled. "As my name is Calen, I swear you'll remember this day!" He laid his mace on the table top and gazed around the jam packed tavern. "Crowded in here, isn't it, folks?" He pointed to the rafters. "You've all heard of the Rising Folk?"

"Sure we have! I even seen one once! So what?"

Calen smiled. "Would it not be wonderful if we, like they, could go up there and find ourselves a better perch?"

"Shut up and sit down, old man!"

"Fetch your creature!"

"You're supposed to show us tricks!"

"And so I shall!" Calen bent to the children. "Rise— now!" he hissed.

The children stood, defiant.

Calen seized the mace and struck it hard across the back of their legs. "Next one's on your kneecaps. Now rise," he repeated.

They rose, straight up, toward the rafters.

Below, a moment's stunned silence, then excited chatter broke out.

Calen tugged the leashes smartly. "Now, dear children," he crooned. "I want you to . . . float; make circles for Uncle Calen."

Mylanfyndra pressed her lips tightly together to keep

from crying. If she could only die, she thought. Right now, this minute. Together she and Brevan floated, dipping gently in the updraughts.

Recovering from their surprise, the tavern folk began to laugh and call out. "Make them do a somersault!"

"Make them dance a jig up there!"

"Make them wash them dirty winders!"

Calen hauled the children down, and to Mylanfyndra's greater shame, he sent them around the room, bobbing over people's heads, to make collection. Folk made fun of them, reaching for them, laughing when they dodged up out of range.

On the way home, the goyar was in a jolly mood. Three times they'd performed, three times the collection cups had filled to overflowing. Back in the house, Calen returned them to the little storeroom, and hitched their shackles to Brok's cage bars. "I'm going out for a while," he said. "Don't try any tricks, or you'll be sorry." He set cups of water on the floor, and went out, locking the door.

His footsteps receded, the outer door banged.

Mylanfyndra bent over, head on her knees.

"I wish," Brevan said dully, "I wish we'd never ever risen."

"Don't say that." Mylanfyndra looked up. Her brother was slumped against the wall, eyes closed, looking totally defeated. "Rising is good and fine. It's a part of us."

"It's brought us nothing but trouble, Myl."

"*People* brought the trouble," she corrected. "But we'll find folk who are not like Toova, and Jag, and Calen."

"You and your bright talk," Brevan snapped. "You get

on my nerves. There are no good people; the whole world is out for itself!"

Mylanfyndra stared. "And you get on mine! You and your gloomy talk! You wallow in misery!" She got out the collar and put it on.

"Myl! What if Calen comes?" Brevan glanced uneasily to the door.

"We'll hear him in plenty of time." She placed both palms over the stone, taking comfort from its familiar cold. She closed her eyes, feeling the stone warm to life. The fire was always waiting, she thought, even when the stone looked dead. "Did you hear today?" she murmured. "Calen asked those people if they'd heard of the Rising Folk."

"So he did, I never thought. I suppose we created quite a stir."

"Yes, but not like on the mesa. They were tickled, Brevan. They weren't afraid of us, and they didn't seem to think us bad. I wonder—"

The door banged again. Mylanfyndra hastily put the collar away, but Calen didn't come in. Pots clattered in the kitchen, the smell of durrerry filtered under the door. At last, Calen brought two bowls, set them down. "Eat," he said. "Then we work."

"At what?" Brevan demanded.

"Learning parlor tricks!" Laughing, Calen went out.

After they had eaten, the goyar led them through the kitchen into a tiny parlor overlooking the alley. "We did well today," he said. "But tonight, we'll do better. The rising's not enough, by itself. The folk called for tricks—and tricks they'll have! So now, let's try—"

A knock came on the door.

"Bother!" Calen went to the window. "It's your lady friend," he said. "You keep quiet, d'you hear?" He went out, locking the door.

Their friend? Mylanfyndra went to the window. "The Toova-woman!"

She heard the door open, heard Calen say "Yes, what do you want?"

"I'm looking for two children. A boy and girl. Have you seen them." The voice was so sweet and friendly, just like Toova's when she spoke with the Elders in the Moot.

"I certainly have not," Calen said. "No children here."

"They came down this alley last night," the woman persisted. "Did you see or hear anything at all?"

"No. Ask elsewhere, good day," Calen said, and shut the door.

For the longest moment, the woman stood, just staring. Then she called out. "Very well, goyar. If you should see them—remember that I came asking." She turned about and walked away toward the square.

Calen came in. "There, you should be grateful I sent her packing," he said, grinning. "What does she want with you, anyway? Would it have something to do with going up in the world? Haha! Don't worry, Uncle Calen will keep you safe. Now: back to work."

For several hours, he drilled them in crude maneuvers to perform in the tavern later that night. All the while, Mylanfyndra raged inside—but said nothing while he wielded the mace.

After supper, Calen put them to rest for an hour or two.

"It's a late crowd," he said. "You'll want to look fresh."

"I shan't do those silly things," Mylanfyndra said, glaring at the door. "I shan't eat or sleep or rise until we've gotten away from that man!"

"But how, in these?" Brevan rattled his chains.

"I don't *know*," she said. "But we'll be free before this night is out!"

The tavern was crammed with people waiting to see the goyar's new act. People stood on tables, lined the walls. At the sight of all those avid faces, Mylanfyndra began to shake. How to avoid a second, worse, round of humiliation? She crouched beside Calen's chair, deep in thought. When she glanced up, the faintest glimmer of an idea came. She looked across to Brevan, their eyes met. "Myl," Brevan whispered. "If we could get a knife, cut through the straps, maybe we could break free and run."

"Maybe," she nodded. "But listen, I have a better idea . . ."

The crowd grew restless and rowdy. A man banged his knife hilt on the tabletop and shouted for the show to start. Others did likewise, and soon the tavern was filled with banging and clapping and stamping.

Through it all, Calen calmly finished his ale, then, when the level of excitement reached a certain pitch, he stood, raising his mace for silence. "Gentle folks, you are about to witness—"

"Get on with it!"

"Cut the cackle!"

"To witness a feat the like of which—"

"I already seen it noontide!"

Undaunted, Calen worked through his pitch. "As my name is Calen, you'll remember this night!" He laid the mace on the table top. "Crowded in here, isn't it?" He pointed to the rafters, his eyes gleaming in the banks of candle flame. "You've heard of the Flying Folk? Wouldn't it be wonderful if we could rise like them and find ourselves a better perch?" He turned his head, hissed to the children.

"Up, now—and remember what I taught you—go up, or I box your ears!"

"That you'll not!" Mylanfyndra yelled, and, snatching up the mace, she brought it down on Calen's knuckles with full force. With a loud cry, the goyar let go their leashes. Mylanfyndra and Brevan shot up into the rafters, shucked their harnesses, and dropped them through the silence onto Calen's upturned face. Then, moving higher, Mylanfyndra swung Calen's stick at the nearest skylight and shattered the dark panes. Glass shards rained down upon the seated patrons. Riot broke out: folk stampeding, upending chairs and tables, spilling ale all over in the rush for the door. More than that, Mylanfyndra didn't see, for, letting fall the goyar's mace, she rose after Brevan, through the open skylight and out into the wide night air.

CHAPTER 20

 "Which way?" Brevan called. "North?"

"We must get the treasure back first."

"The treasure? Oh, Myl. We don't know where Calen's house is."

"We might," Mylanfyndra argued. "If we find the marketplace." Although they had come and gone sealed up in the cart, she remembered the alley lay on the shadowed side of the moonlit square. She circled high to take her bearings. Like the warehouse district on the mesa, this lowly quarter was away from the main center. But the town was not so big. It did not take long to locate the moonlit space. "It's all right," she called to Brevan, who was lagging behind. "There's no one down there."

"Not that we can *see*," Brevan conceded.

Mylanfyndra landed on the cobbles, ducked under the

shadowed gables, trying not to feel irritated, trying to avoid another row. "Here, Brevan," she beckoned. "The alley's right here."

"We're taking a risk, Myl. Calen will be back." He landed beside her, peering doubtfully into the darkness of the alley.

"Not until we're done. We *flew*, Brevan. Oh, don't come then, but I'll not leave that stuff for Calen!" Mylanfyndra took off down the alley, to the goyar's house with its telltale pole. Finding Calen's door unlocked, she ran through the kitchen into the storeroom behind. Against Brok's shrill chatter, Mylanfyndra snatched up the treasure bag and fled, colliding with Brevan on the doorstep. "The Toova-woman's back that way—" He pointed breathlessly back toward the alley's blind end. "Run for the marketplace!"

They ran.

"Are you sure?" Mylanfyndra glanced over her shoulder. "I can't hear anything."

"She came after me," Brevan gasped. "She must have been waiting near the corner. When you left . . . she just popped out of nowhere." Brevan took big, puffy breaths. "When we got to Calen's, lucky . . . you'd gone . . . inside. I led her past . . . down to the end . . . then I turned around and *pooosh!* I knocked her down and ran!"

Mylanfyndra fixed her eyes on the moonlit square only paces away. "Well, she won't catch us now."

"But I will!" Calen stepped out, stick raised, blocking the alley entrance. "To think I'd lost you, and here you are for the second time—" He halted, frowning. "Now why would you come back here . . . aha!" he cried, spying the pouch in Mylanfyndra's hand. She tried to dodge past, but Calen seized her wrist and held on.

"Let her go!" Brevan rushed him, ramming his middle. With a grunt of pain, Calen straightened up and lashed out at Brevan with his mace. "You'll pay for that."

"Oh? Think again, goyar!" Mylanfyndra cried, and kicked out.

"Ow! Ow!" Calen let go, clutching at his shins.

"Come on, Brevan!" Mylanfyndra ran from the alley and rose into the air. But Brevan did not follow. He lay on the cobbles, Calen over him, leering triumphantly out into the square. "What now, girl? See: I have your brother!" He pulled a harness from his coat pocket and shook it out.

As Calen bent to fit the harness, Mylanfyndra eyed Calen's back, remembering Jag. She kicked the wind and plummeted as before. Speed was the trick. To dive fast, take him off guard . . . The instant before impact, he spun about, grabbed her ankles, and held on with a grasp strong as vine. Mylanfyndra drew back her arm and rapped him smartly with the treasure pouch.

Calen almost let go—but not quite. "Aha, let's see that," he cried. Freeing one hand, he wrenched the pouch from her grasp.

"Leave it, let me free!" Mylanfyndra cried, twisting about. But to her horror, the goyar shook loose the drawstring and peered inside. Mylanfyndra ceased to breathe. Another moment and this evil man would touch the shining, golden secrets! She raised her head and shouted. "Help! Help! We're being robbed!"

Out of nowhere, a whirlwind hit, sending Calen reeling,

throwing Mylanfyndra to the ground. Calen dropped the pouch with a yell and took off across the square, not looking back. Mylanfyndra stayed put, her arms crossed over her head. That whirlwind: what terrible force had unleashed it?

"Are you all right, my dear?"

Mylanfyndra lifted her head carefully. Standing over her with anxious face—the Toova-woman!

The woman reached under Mylanfyndra's arms and sat her up. "There, there. Don't be afraid. I am your friend," she said in a soothing voice. "Just you sit while I look to your brother." Before Mylanfyndra could say a word, the woman turned to Brevan, and felt his cheek. Then she took from some pocket a small vial. She shook it, removed the stopper, and held the open vial under Brevan's nose. He squeezed his eyes, sucked in a long, shuddering breath, and sneezed. Nodding in satisfaction, the woman restoppered the vial and put it away. Then she patted Brevan's cheek. "Come on, my lad. Let's get you moving." She looked to Mylanfyndra, who still sat watching, utterly confused. "Up, young woman. Go stand by the corner and keep an eye out for that scoundrel goyar."

Mylanfyndra pulled herself together. "He won't be back," she said, climbing unsteadily to her feet.

"You think not? Well, think again," the woman said firmly. "If that rogue saw what was in the pouch, he's gone for reinforcements!" She turned back to Brevan, who was sitting up and rubbing his head.

The pouch. Still lying where Calen had dropped it, a tip of gold poking from the neck. Mylanfyndra scooped it up quickly, tightened the drawstring, and restored it to its usual hiding place. Now she went to the corner and gazed out across the square. *How had the woman known about the pouch?* No time to wonder. Boots clattered on the cobbles, a knot of men burst into the square, headed for the alley. "Calen's back!" she cried.

The woman took Brevan's arm calmly. "Young man. Can you stand?"

Brevan half-rose, and sat down again with a bump.

The men were coming fast. In another moment, they'd be here, and the alley would be blocked. Mylanfyndra darted to Brevan's side—too late! The men reached the corner, and Calen came at them with a loud, triumphant cry.

"Rise," the woman commanded quietly.

"But what about—"

"Now."

Something in the woman's voice made Mylanfyndra obey, made her rise and leave Brevan behind on the ground. What, was she mad? she thought in a sudden panic. Whirling, she saw the woman gather Brevan in her arms—and rise up after!

"This way," the woman called, as they reached the silvered chimney tops. Cradling Brevan firmly to her bosom, the majestic figure rose higher, then struck out north, over the town. In a daze, Mylanfyndra followed, Calen's shouts dwindling below. Not until they were out of Ludder's End did the woman slow and spiral down. "Here we are, my lad." She lowered Brevan gently onto the scrubby ground.

He was fully awake now, and trembling violently.

"Shock," the woman said, taking off her mantle and settling it about his shoulders. "The goyar caught you a nasty blow. You'll have a headache for a bit. But it will pass." She smiled. "So: finally we meet."

Mylanfyndra stared, still dumbfounded. She thought of the slender, graceful figure etched on the medallion, hair streaming, and lightning streaking from the heels. "You— you rose, like us." This huge woman who could scarce run five yards without getting puffed—one of those golden folk?

"Indeed I did," the woman laughed. "And pity on us all if I had not." She crossed her arms over her chest and dipped her head. "Permit me to introduce myself: I am Yoleyna, athlynder-skyrr."

Athlynder-skyrr?

"May I—the pouch, please?" Yoleyna held out her hand.

Mylanfyndra folded her arms over her apron protectively.

Yoleyna smiled. "It is quite safe, child. Here, see." She pulled down her shawl, revealing a golden collar just like Mylanfyndra's, its amber throat clasp alight with inner flame. *"My* thruyl," she said.

"Threy?" Brevan echoed, catching the woman's accent.

"The thruyl of the athlynder-skyrr. As for your fremma—" Yoleyna reached under her shawl—and pulled out a pouch just like theirs, if somewhat older and shabbier. She loosened the drawstring and shook out a medallion, and a small, gold cylinder, just like theirs, also.

"Athlynder-skyrr," Mylanfyndra pronounced carefully, staring down at the pouch and its contents. She looked up. "Our pouch—*fremma:* it belonged to one of your athlynder-skyrr?"

"Yes."

Mylanfyndra slowly unhitched the fremma and placed it in Yoleyna's hands. To her surprise, Yoleyna made no move to open it. Instead, the woman simply sat, head bowed over the weathered leather bag. When she looked up at last, there were tears on her cheeks. "So you really are," Yoleyna said, her voice so low Mylanfyndra scarcely heard her.

"Are what? Really are what?" Brevan demanded loudly.

Yoleyna sighed. "Alive, my dears."

"Of course we're alive," Mylanfyndra said, then realized that although the woman had told her name, she and Brevan had not extended like courtesy. "We're sorry, but with all the excitement we haven't introduced ourselves. My name is—"

"Mylanfyndra," said Yoleyna solemnly. "And he is Brevalan."

CHAPTER 21

 The children cried out together. "How did you know?"

"It's *Brevan,* not Brevalan," Mylanfyndra added.

"Brevan?" Yoleyna reached into their pouch and withdrew the two small strips of gold. She straightened them and held them out, embossed sides up. She examined them carefully, then gave one strip to Mylanfyndra, the other to Brevan. She pointed to Mylanfyndra's strip. "This says 'Mylanfyndra', and this"—she tapped Brevan's—"says 'Brev-a-lan'."

The children looked at each other. "What are they?" Brevan demanded.

"They're your baby tags, put on your wrists the day you were born."

The day they were born? But— "How do you *know?*"

Mylanfyndra curled the strip around and around her finger. "Who are we? What do they mean?"

" 'Mylanfyndra' means 'windbairn'; 'child of the air'."

"And 'Brevan'?"

" 'Brevalan'," Yoleyna corrected. "Although we'll keep to 'Brevan' for now, if you like. It means 'skytreader'." She turned to Brevan. "Are you ready to go on now, Skytreader?"

"Where to?"

"Home, to Falath-coom."

"Home?" Mylanfyndra echoed.

Yoleyna smiled. "Believe me, there will be more rejoicing when we arrive than you could dream. For full eleven years we've thought you dead."

"Who's 'we'?" asked Mylanfyndra, but Brevan overrode her.

"How did you find us? How will you let them know?"

"Through the thruyl." Yoleyna drew the collar from their pouch and held it up. "Which of you wears it?"

"Myl does," Brevan said.

Yoleyna opened it out. "Here, put it on, Mylanfyndra. Fire the beacon and tell them you're coming home."

Home! Mylanfyndra closed her eyes. She felt the metal on her neck, the coldness of the thruyl. She cupped the stone thoughtfully, until Brevan cried out. "Aha, I see! When a stone lights up, you know it, somehow."

"Yes, but in your case, since you do not know how to use the thruyl, we couldn't tell who was wearing it, only that it was athlynder-skyrr, for only we can light the stone. Neither could we learn where you were, for the signals were too brief to pinpoint. But when they traveled north, I came to find you. When you and I converged on Ludder's End last night, there would have been one happy ending but for Calen. Never mind, here we are, and all is well. Tell me, I'm bursting to know: where *have* you come from, Brevan?"

"From the Gansor—off a mesa, though I wouldn't know which one."

"The *Gansor?*" Yoleyna shook her head. "No one can live in the thermal region—at least, that's what we thought—ah! Your stone has just lit up, Mylanfyndra. Two signals now," she said, tapping her own. "Two in the one place. The coom will be fairly buzzing! Shall we rise?"

Shall we rise? Mylanfyndra shook her head as though to clear it. This woman, and the names: windbairn, and sky-treader! Who would give babies such names but folk to whom rising was a perfectly ordinary, normal thing! She got to her feet excitedly. "You're what they call the Rising Folk!"

"Where is this Falath-coom?" Brevan asked. "How far is it?"

"It lies to the north, many days travel, for normal folk. But for athlynder-skyrr, it's one night and one day from here."

"What's it like?"

Many days travel, for normal folk! Mylanfyndra was readily forgetting the inconvenience of going around on foot. "What I would like to know," she said, but at that Yoleyna threw up her hands. "Mercy! Do we rise and get there with good speed, or sit here all night discussing it?" She collected their baby tags and dropped them into the fremma. But not the thruyl. "You keep that signal going, Mylanfyndra,

171

loud and clear!" Yoleyna said, handing back the pouch. Mylanfyndra stowed it resignedly. Her questions would have to wait, it seemed. At Yoleyna's gesture, she and Brevan went to stand on either side of her, then, firmly joining hands, they rose and headed north, leaving Ludder's End behind.

Hand in hand, with Yoleyna in between, they pressed on steadily. Mylanfyndra was glad of the woman's powerful pull, for the headwinds were strong, and she was tired. She glanced across to Brevan. His head drooped, his eyes were shut. Asleep? She studied him curiously. How could he be on such a journey! *Home, to Falath-coom* . . .

She thought back to the mesa. It had been their whole world. Now it was left behind, the past gone to ashes. And she and Brevan went on to folk with whom they belonged—and not just for rising. Yoleyna had *recognized* her and Brevan, she reminded herself. This woman had known them as babies . . .

Those name tags, part of the treasure—*theirs!* She realized with a jolt that Gven had known it all along; and he had let the townsfolk think them mesa children to protect some greater truth. When he found them, were they with someone else—the one to whom the fremma belonged? Yes—else how would he have learned their proper given names? Gven could not possibly have read the tags. Someone must have told him!

Mylanfyndra touched the glowing stone, her heart racing.

Gven's made-up tales: did they contain some grain of truth? A clue to what really happened? Those many tales of Breia: she and Brevan had taken so much comfort from them. But lie like that, why, it seemed such a cruel thing, yet Gven was the kindest, gentlest, and most honest man on all the mesa. So why invent a parent who never was— and make it the *mother*, at that? She could have been the one he met that night. If so—*where was she now?*

Impatience surged, a will—a need—to learn the truth. It got so bad Mylanfyndra had to squeeze her eyes tight against it. Gven said Breia died. Had their real mother died also? She must *know*, and yet she was afraid. Better wait, she thought. Do as Yoleyna said. Mylanfyndra eyed the woman's profile covertly. How could they have called her the Toova-woman!

The bluff night winds struck through, making Mylanfyndra shudder.

"Cold?" Yoleyna squeezed Mylanfyndra's hand.

"A little," she answered, trying to keep her teeth from chattering.

"I'm not surprised. We've been flying for the best part of the night. You must be hungry, and tired. Never mind, we'll stop after the sun comes up—which won't be too long now. Meantime, close your eyes, let go."

Reassured, Mylanfyndra obeyed, feeling the woman's powerful grip take over. Her eyes began to close, her breathing deepened. . . .

Brevan's shout awoke her. "Look, Myl!"

The sun was up, slanting its rays sidewise across flat, brown terrain that stretched all around them. Way ahead, silver winked on the horizon.

"Like the well in the charnon," Mylanfyndra remarked.

"Well?" Yoleyna looked puzzled. "There are no wells in the desert. Oh, you must have found an oasis."

"O-asis?"

"I'm forgetting," Yoleyna said. "There is no ready water on the mesas. Nor much of anything else."

"If that is not a well," Mylanfyndra persisted, "and not an oasis, pray what is it?"

"Lake Kemal," Yoleyna answered. "A stretch of water big enough to drown your whole mesa."

Mylanfyndra stared ahead blankly.

Yoleyna smiled. "It must indeed be difficult for you to comprehend, coming from that barren place. What can grow there?"

"Oh, plenty." Mylanfyndra told of the market gardeners, the root crops harvested before the glair. Then she described the podliths, and the creeping stoneflowers that in the summer webbed the moist, gray doft.

"*Gray* clay?" Yoleyna looked sharp. "You are in the gray region? No wonder we have never seen you."

"What do you mean, gray region?" Brevan said.

"I know," Mylanfyndra cut in, watching the silver speck grow to a shimmer. "The mesas in the Gansor are mostly red, but there's a bunch of gray ones, isn't there? But I never saw another gray one like ours, only a red and gray one next to it. So our mesa must be just inside the gray region—well, not too far inside it," she amended, remembering that she had drifted one whole day and night before she saw anything save mist.

"Why is it no wonder you haven't seen our mesa?" Brevan said.

"The Gansor is a kind of giant desert, and we believed it to be wholly uninhabited, as I said. We do not cross it save to get from one place to another, and your gray region is way off the beaten skytracks."

"Skytracks?"

"Skytracks, skylanes, skyroads—major windcurrents." Yoleyna looked up. "Although you cannot see them, the main prevailing winds form paths in the sky just as plain as those on the ground."

"Yes, yes!" Mylanfyndra cried. "I know. I rode one north. Brevan must have ridden it, too, for we both came to the same place on the Edge."

Yoleyna looked very pleased. "Indeed. Except that you must have taken two roads, not one. Since your gray region lies west of the north-south skyways, you must have ridden one current east, until it fed into the main northern skyway. There are many minor crosscurrents such as yours, none of which we take, having had no reason to—or so we thought." She shook her head. "We had no idea, no idea. And I cannot imagine how your folk got there in the first place. Or how they manage to survive! My poor, dear children, take heart: you have many treats ahead: lakes, like that one coming up. More than that, you'll see rivers, canals, streams—and even an ocean." As the woman described them, and hinted at the wealth of plants and trees and flowers that they nurtured, Mylanfyndra sighed. "Poor Ebbwe. She would have loved to hear of all these growing things."

"Ebbwe?"

"Our friend," Mylanfyndra said. "If it weren't for her, we wouldn't be here. She saved our lives."

"Goodness! How was that? And—look, maybe you'd

better start at the beginning. Where did you live? Who took care of you and brought you up?"

Her eyes fixed on the nearing lake, Mylanfyndra told of Gven. Of the good life lived until his sickness.

"What a fine, remarkable man," Yoleyna exclaimed. "To have kept you safe all this long time! And he fell helpless, you say? What happened then?"

Brevan gave a gist of the terrible things that happened after. Then Mylanfyndra spoke of their rising, their discovery and trial. "The people were afraid of us. They called us evil. Sick. Wyrth-possessed: the wyrth are supposed to be mist-spirits, you see. I knew it wasn't true because rising felt so normal and good."

"But breaking out with no one by to explain? Weren't you terrified? Didn't you wonder whether the folk might not be right?"

"I did," Brevan said. "I did all the time, even when I didn't say so."

"Brevan!"

"It's all right, Mylanfyndra," Yoleyna said. "It's perfectly natural to feel that way. Oh, my dears, what you must have gone through! After that awful trial, what then?"

Mylanfyndra told of the cage, and Ebbwe's rescuing them. And as she spoke, Yoleyna's face grew grave. "Truly," she said. "Those folk have much to learn—and learn they shall, I promise you." She pressed the children to her, squashing the breath out of them. "Never mind," she went on, releasing them. "From now on things will improve! Look, we're almost to the lake now."

"It must be the biggest in all the world," Mylanfyndra

said, gazing ahead to rippling waves that stretched clear to the horizon.

"Indeed no," Yoleyna told them. "Kemal is the least of the Nine Great Lakes. We live by the waters of Falath, the greatest of them all. Would you stop here, or on Kemal's shore?"

"The shore!" the children cried together.

They sped on, but as they neared the lake, the children pulled back, gazing down. Directly below, the ground was stippled with green dots, sparse at first, then growing denser. "Trees," Yoleyna explained. "That's my favorite orchard village."

"What's an orchard village?"

"Oh, goodness, Mylanfyndra. An orchard is a grove of fruit trees. A village is a tiny town. This one's call Ulfrond, or Place of Plenty."

"Oh, how lovely!" Mylanfyndra gazed down on pale pastel smudges in amongst the green. Houses painted pink, and mauve, and yellow, and blue, delicate as the morning sky. Through their midst curved a shining arc, like a wand of silvered leoia. Brevan pointed. "Is that a river?"

"Canal. To water those." On either side of the canal, fruit trees stretched away in tidy, uniform ranks.

"They're nothing like the squishy fruit trees by the oasis," Mylanfyndra remarked. "These are shorter and bushier." And lacking the plumes.

"The trees in the charnon are tropical plants, with soft, tropical fruits—Traveler's Boon, we call them. The trees below us are what you'll find in these colder northern parts. You've missed blossom time," Yoleyna went on. "But you'll not have so long to wait for fruit. Let's take a closer look." She drew the children toward the village.

As they neared, Mylanfyndra saw folk with buckets going to and from the canal, which, as she now saw, was lined with steep, high ridges. "Why those piles of dirt along the canal? Seems a lot of work to climb over them every time you need fresh water."

"It is," Yoleyna agreed. "But without those levees, come the rainy season the canal would overflow and flood the village." As she spoke, a woman in billowing skirts and apron looked up and waved, calling out.

The children pulled back, tugging on Yoleyna's hands, but Yoleyna held them steady. "Fusci and I are old friends. She's merely bidding us good morning." Yoleyna let go now and moved lower. *"I'm in a rush right now, Fusci!"* she yelled. *"But I'll be by in a day or two!* Poor Fusci," Yoleyna said, rising again and rejoining hands. "Her son has just got wed, and now she's lonely in her empty house—she such a loving soul. Oh, look, the rest are waving now."

Indeed, all the other villagers were gazing up, smiling and waving.

"Good morning!" Brevan shouted, growing bold. "Nice day!"

"They look so friendly. And they seem to know you," Mylanfyndra said.

"Indeed," Yoleyna said. "I pass over Ulfrond often. I even spend the night here when the weather turns bad."

"Might we, sometime?" Mylanfyndra said wistfully, reluctant to leave such manifest good will.

Yoleyna smiled. "Perhaps."

———

They landed beside the lake. Mylanfyndra stared across the water in fascination. Why, on the ground, she could scarcely see the farther shore!

Mylanfyndra and Brevan knelt at the water's edge and drank greedily.

"I'm so hungry." Brevan pulled out a wizened squishy fruit, well past its time. "We could share this," he said, doubtfully.

"That won't be necessary." From her fremma, Yoleyna produced her golden cylinder. "This is our medron," she

said. She twisted off the cap and withdrew what looked like sticks of fine broomstraw. "Here." She gave one to each of the children. "This will fill the hole."

"What is it?" Mylanfyndra took hers, twirled it between her fingers.

"Waybread for a hungry traveler."

Brevan bit. "Tastes dry, but good."

Mylanfyndra nibbled the end off hers, recalling the fine grains she had shaken from their cylinder. Had that been waybread, too? Gone to dust after . . . "The athlynder-skyrr: who—what are they?"

"They are sky-messengers, my dear. And keepers of the lore."

Sky-messengers! "What about Falath-coom?"

"As I said, it's our home—and fortress."

"What's a fortress?" Brevan asked.

"A place of safety, young man."

"So folk hunt you down, too," Mylanfyndra said quickly.

"Agh, folk do not hunt athlynder-skyrr," Yoleyna said. "They would not be so foolish. But once they did, and then the world was sorry."

"Why? When? How?"

"In the far time, athlynder-skyrr were highly honored for their calling, but after a time, they became taken for granted, even abused by the ruling Houses."

"How?"

"Well, if their message or finding displeased an House, they would be punished, or held hostage, or even sometimes put to death. It got so bad that in the end the few survivors fled north to Falath-byr—the lake valley—and built the coom."

"The Houses must have been put out," Brevan said.

"Oh, yes. The world came to a virtual stop. The ruling Houses laid siege to the coom."

"But how silly," Mylanfyndra cried. "Athlynder-skyrr could come and go over their heads at will!"

Yoleyna smiled. "Exactly. By the first snows, we had a treaty. Athlynder-skyrr would serve again, but only as a free people."

Mylanfyndra held up their medallion. "Is this athlynder-skyrr?" She pointed to the flying figure.

"Aye." Yoleyna pulled her own medallion. "This is our horm." She held it out, flying figure up. "This is our symbol. The lightning from the hands represents knowledge. The spikes from the feet speak of our speed."

"And the other side?"

Yoleyna turned her horm over. Etched on its face was a profile; finer, younger, but unmistakably their companion.

"This side serves as personal seal, and proof of our identity."

Mylanfyndra held out their horm profile up. "Who was she, then?"

Yoleyna, suddenly a-bustle, reached for her fremma and put her horm away. "That you'll learn in Falath-coom."

"Why not now?"

"My, look at that sun." Yoleyna climbed heavily to her feet. "Time's racing: shall we be on our way?"

CHAPTER 22

Yoleyna shook Mylanfyndra awake. "We're home. Look, there's the byr!"

As they touched ground, Mylanfyndra became aware of tremendous noise, all around: insects clicking, chirping, whirring—a wash of night sound. Something burst from the dark in a brittle of wings, blundered onto Mylanfyndra's cheek, then shot off, calling loudly. Tee-*kwee!* tee-*kwee!* tee-*kweeeee!*

"What was *that?*" Mylanfyndra rubbed the tickle it had left.

"A tiqui." Yoleyna pointed up. "In the trees: hundreds of them."

Hundreds? Mylanfyndra was gazing up when three figures approached, two of them bearing torches, flames shredding in the wind. The third, a gaunt, elderly man with upright bearing stepped out to take Yoleyna's hands. "So, Seeker: we were hoping you'd make it tonight."

"Allow me to present our foundlings, Wurthen." Yoleyna led the children forward. "This is Brevan—Brevalan, as we know him; and this is Mylanfyndra."

Wurthen eyed them gravely, his gaze coming to rest on Mylanfyndra's thruyl. She raised her hand protectively, dropped it as he smiled and nodded. "Yes, yes, I see." He turned and beckoned. "Eothelwyn? Althya?"

The other two stepped up: a younger man and a woman. The man was middling tall, burly and broad under his night mantle. "Eothelwyn, Recorder, welcomes you to Falath-coom," he said, in a strong, warm voice. He slipped off his hood, and a mass of wiry hair sprang out about his shoulders.

"I, Althya, Reader, welcome you also," the woman said. Reaching barely higher than Mylanfyndra, her pale, delicate face framed by long, dark locks drawn back looked perfectly beautiful in the torchlight. She scanned their faces, then turned to Wurthen. "Counselor: they are exhausted. We should continue the welcome tomorrow."

Wurthen nodded. "As you say. Mylanfyndra and Brevalan, it is mainly hard to let you go so soon, but Althya is right. Yoleyna—get them to bed."

"Certainly, Wurthen." Yoleyna led Mylanfyndra and Brevan away, under a gated arch into a fragrant garden, loud with tiquis and other night sounds.

"Where are we?" Mylanfyndra looked warily about. Paths led off in all directions, disappearing around bushes and under trees.

"Crossing the garth—our main courtyard," Yoleyna said.

"The coom encloses it around—you'll see tomorrow. Your quarters are in the children's wing at the rear. It's where you will eat, play—and also learn."

"I have learned much already," Brevan cried. "I can see what a great fortress the coom makes with the gates shut. Nobody can enter, yet you enjoy fresh air and come and go easily, rising from this open space."

Mylanfyndra faltered as a huge figure of a man loomed, looking down upon them, blocking their way. Head and shoulders above Yoleyna, he was shrouded in a cloak, hood pulled well down over his head.

"It's all right, Mylanfyndra," Yoleyna said. "It's but a statue, see?" She rapped her knuckles on the mantle's rigid folds. "This is Umfahlan, the coom's founder. This stone likeness marks his grave."

"Grave?"

"Athlynder-skyrr are buried here in the garth—it is our way."

"A good way," Brevan said. "On the mesa, they throw the dead off the cliffs."

Except for Gven, thought Mylanfyndra, saying nothing.

They moved on, passing at last under a cloistered porch, through a deep doorway into a long, straight passage leading left and right. "Left lies the school, where you will do all your lessons—except for skyrring, of course."

The children cried out together. "Skyrring?"

"Riding the airs." Yoleyna steered them right. "The dormitories lie this way, and the guest rooms—where you'll stay this night."

Dormitories. Mylanfyndra thought of the brug. "We—we all sleep together?"

184

"You'll sleep with the girls and Brevan, with the boys."
Mylanfyndra drew in to Brevan's side. "You mean we'll
be *separated?*"

"It is our way," Yoleyna said gravely. "I see the idea
disturbs you."

"Indeed it does," Mylanfyndra said. "You can't part us."

"These dormitories, can we see them?" Brevan said.

"Why certainly." Yoleyna led them down the passage a
way, then opened a door to their left. Neat cots lined a
narrow, whitewashed room, their covers bright against the
walls. Beside each cot, stood a small chest of drawers. "The
boys dormitory," Yoleyna explained. "As you see, you each
have your private locker. See the door at the far end?" In
the middle of the rear wall. "The washrooms—baths, show-
ers, and whatnot. The girls quarters are much the same,
Mylanfyndra."

"It looks nice," Brevan said. "You should see the brug!"

Mylanfyndra surveyed the room stiffly, trying to picture
herself in the girls dormitory, lying alone among strangers
and no Brevan. Why, they had always stood together, had
taken their strength and courage from each other. These
coom children: what if she didn't like them? *What if they
didn't like her?*

"They're at supper now," Yoleyna was saying. "When
they learn about you, they'll be so excited, you'll likely *hear*
them—though you'll not see them now till morning." She
led them on to a door at the end of the passage. "Here we
are: the guest rooms. As I just said, we are putting you in
here for tonight, at least, being so new to everything." She
ushered them into a small sitting room lit with tall tapers.
Despite her agitation, Mylanfyndra noted the bright, flow-

ered couch, deep chairs, and shiny white table ringed with high-backed seats. A fire burned in the far wall. On either side of the hearth, a small window stood open to the dark and noisy garth. On the right lay two small cells, each with a cot, the farther one having a window. On the left was a tiny room with washstand, jugs of hot water, a stack of towels, and clean nightshirts.

"This is a truly wondrous place!" Brevan cried, bouncing out an easy chair. Mylanfyndra hung back inside the door, unbending; impatient to have Yoleyna gone and Brevan alone.

"Twenty minutes to clean up," Yoleyna said. "Then I bring supper."

"They can't part us like this!" Mylanfyndra declared, the instant Yoleyna had gone. "How could she let them!"

Brevan poked his head into the nearer bedroom. "It's their way, Myl. They won't change things just for us. You can have the window, if you want."

"Thanks," she answered shortly. Wasn't he bothered at all? Didn't he mind how upset she was?

"And you can wash first, too."

"Wash?" Her voice was shrill. "I won't wash! I won't anything until this is settled."

Brevan shrugged. "Suit yourself. But I'm not standing around for long in this state."

Mylanfyndra turned on her heel and went into the washroom, shutting the door behind her. She stripped off her grimy clothes, and angrily set to with soap and washcloth. As she scrubbed, her anger began to subside. Her first real bathe since the brug—since Gven died, to tell the truth.

She rubbed herself down with the brisky towels, her skin tingling pleasantly all over. Then she shook out a nightshirt and slipped it on, feeling its roughness, catching a whiff of wind and sun. Feeling better now despite herself, she went outside to let Brevan take his turn.

Mylanfyndra stood by the hearth for a while, staring into the flames. This room stirred up feelings, memories of former bedtimes; she and Brevan on one side of the hut, Gven in his opposite corner. Nights like this, she'd fall asleep against the sound of Gven and Brevan breathing; content, secure . . .

Abruptly, she crossed from hearth to casement.

The air pulsed with tiquis. Strange new scents blew in from unseen night blooms. Mylanfyndra leaned out, reaching for the flowers beneath the window, stroked them with her fingertips, thinking. If only things had not gone wrong! Behind her, Brevan splashed noisily, humming a tune. Her throat shrank up. How could these people part them? And how could Brevan let them? Tightfaced, Mylanfyndra left the window and threw herself down on the couch.

Just as Brevan came out all scrubbed and shiny, Yoleyna entered with a loaded tray. "My, you're certainly looking better," she said. She set the tray on the table and pointed down. "A light supper, so close to bedtime. Fruit and toasted meal cakes. This"—she pointed to a bowl of sweet, sticky delight—"is squishy preserve. Sit—enjoy," she said, and went to the door.

"Aren't you eating with us?" Brevan said.

Yoleyna smiled. "Surely you'd like some time alone? Don't worry, I'll be back to put out your lights and tuck you in."

"No, wait," Mylanfyndra called, but the door had already closed.

Brevan attacked the cakes, scattering crumbs all over. Mylanfyndra picked up a shiny, yellow fruit and put it on her plate.

Children's voices sounded down the passage. Footsteps running, quickly shushed. Mylanfyndra ran to the door, peeked out, Brevan at her shoulder. Four grown-ups were shepherding the children into the dormitories. A girl glanced their way and called out, pointing. Mylanfyndra and Brevan dodged back, shutting the door. They stood, holding their breath, waiting for someone to come and scold them. More laughter. A door banged. Then quiet.

"Can they all rise, I wonder?" Brevan said.

"Why else would they be here?" Mylanfyndra opened the door again, looking out. The passage was deserted now.

Brevan went back to the table. "Come on, Myl. Eat up."

"I'm not hungry."

"Look, Myl. We'll talk to Yoleyna when she comes back," he said. "Meantime, you're here, aren't you? Isn't this what you wanted?"

"Yes, but—" Mylanfyndra fetched the thruyl from the washroom and replaced it around her neck. It wasn't just their being parted. There were the questions, and she afraid of answers . . .

Yoleyna came in. "Mylanfyndra, haven't you eaten *anything?*"

"I can't," Mylanfyndra said. "Yoleyna—can we stay with you? Brevan and I together?"

"Oh, my. Wurthen said we'd deal with this tomorrow." Yoleyna piled the things onto the tray. "You, dear one, are very, very tired; more tired than you know. All this really had best be left till morning," she said, and gathered up the tray.

"I won't go to bed. I won't sleep. I won't *breathe!*" Mylanfyndra declared, then, without warning, began to cry.

Yoleyna set down the tray, and hurried over. "There, there," she said. She put her arms about Mylanfyndra, wrapping her in warmth. "Hold on: I'll see what I can do." Letting go, she scooped up the tray, and strode out.

"Why!" Brevan exploded, as soon as the door was closed. "Why do you have to stir up this fuss! What will they think of us now?"

Mylanfyndra rounded on him. "Don't you care at all?"

"Of course I do," he said, then added, "What about, exactly?"

"About . . . oh, lots of things. Like who we are, and what they're going to do with us."

"They already told us," Brevan answered. "And they said they'd tell us more tomorrow."

"Tomorrow?" Mylanfyndra said scornfully. "I'll know *now.*"

Yoleyna brought Eothelwyn and Althya.

"Let's sit ourselves down," Althya said calmly, going to the table. "Which of you would speak first?"

"Not me," Brevan said, dragging out a chair. "Myl's the one who's kicking up."

Mylanfyndra glared at him, but he kept his eyes averted. She scraped back a seat, sat herself down. "What's this about separating Brevan and me?"

"They are upset about the dormitories," Yoleyna said.

"*Myl's* upset," Brevan amended.

"As is understandable," Althya said. "Look, this separation: it's only for sleeping. You'll get used to it, everyone does."

Mylanfyndra shook her head slightly.

"But you will, and must, my dear." She paused, surveying Mylanfyndra earnestly across the table. "The fact is you are born to be athlynder-skyrr. You must learn separation sometime."

"How do you mean?"

Althya glanced to Eothelwyn. "We are only making the child more anxious," she said.

"Althya speaks of years from now," Eothelwyn explained. "She refers to the principle of service that all of us must learn. And that is definitely best left to its proper time and place. Mylanfyndra, we understand your feelings, and we also respect them. On this account, you two may bide together in these rooms a while longer, if you like." At his nod, the three grown-ups pushed back their chairs.

"Wait, please. That's not all." Ignoring Brevan's frantic signals, Mylanfyndra laid the horm on the table, profile up. "Who was she?"

Althya eyed her keenly. "I think you know."

"It was our mother, I think." Mylanfyndra shivered.

"Mother!"

"Indeed, Brevan." Eothelwyn spoke up. "Breialynda, she was called. Athlynder-skyrr of the sixth and highest order."

The room seemed to vanish, leaving only the ring of faces in the tapers' light. Breialynda . . . *Breia.* Gven's grain of truth. "Tell us about her—please?"

Althya looked to Yoleyna, who nodded.

"After you were born, Mylanfyndra, your mother went on a mission to An-telfyra. Since her folk lived there, she had a mind to take you both and visit. She left well before the glair, so all should have been fine. But that year, the storms came early, and off the usual tracks." Althya bowed her head.

"We searched the skylanes from end to end," Eothelwyn said. "But when the thruyl's signal failed, we assumed she had died, and you with her."

She had died! Mylanfyndra's soul cried out.

Silence settled on the room.

"That will be all for now, I think," Yoleyna said quietly, her tone brooking no nonsense. Eothelwyn and Althya took their leave and went.

Mylanfyndra suffered herself to be led into her cot and tucked in. But as Yoleyna reached the door, she called out. "Where are you going? Where will you be?"

Yoleyna came back to stand beside her. "Where you'll be in no time, I hope, Mylanfyndra. In the land of dreams." To Mylanfyndra's surprise, the woman perched heavily on the edge of the cot and, leaning over, kissed her cheek. "Remember, my dear: you're home now. The bad times are over, you're safe. But tonight, if you should need me, I'm not far away. Just open the door and call. Someone will fetch me, all right?"

Mylanfyndra nodded. Even so, as Yoleyna made to close the door, she called out. "Leave it open, please? And Brevan's, too?"

She heard Yoleyna bid Brevan goodnight, heard Brevan's

muffled reply. She listened to the woman moving quietly about, blowing out the tapers, raking the fire. "Sleep well, children," Yoleyna called, then left.

Dying embers shifted. Something creaked.

Mylanfyndra lay, staring at the open window. Breia-lynda—Breia . . .

She thought back to the day she and Brevan were swept like ash plumes, over the town, then up into the podlithra. She pictured Breia, brushed by scorching winds, clutching her two babes, falling, falling . . .

When Gven found her, she must have been near death.

Mylanfyndra lay, listening to the sounds from the open window.

Chee-chee; chee-chee; chee-chee.

Bee-tck! Bee-tck! Bee-tck!

Tee-*kwee!* Tee-*kwee!* Tee-*kwee!*

"Brevan?" she called. No reply. Only the familiar sound of deep and rhythmic breathing through the open door.

She sighed, looked to the window, and saw two small, bright stars enclosed within its frame:

Home.

CHAPTER 23

The next morning, Mylanfyndra awoke to a light rapping sound. A girl's face, small and round with large, round eyes was framed in the window.

"Hello, how are you?" the girl said, as Mylanfyndra came up onto one elbow. Before Mylanfyndra could reply, the girl went on, running her words together in one breathless rush, no space between. "I'm Kori. How old are you? I'm ten. I broke out six months ago, but Yoleyna found me only three weeks back. That's her job since she retired from active service, did you know? Finding athlynder-skyrr, I mean. She goes all over the world, she's very good at it and so she should be because she used to be a Pathfinder. When did you break out, did you break out together? I was terrified, of course, until Yoleyna found me. You're very famous, did you know? Everyone's dying to meet you. I've been trying to wake you for hours. I threw stones, but that didn't work, so I tried knocking. I even called your name. I was beginning to think that you were dead! *Please* come out, quick, so we can meet before the bell. Because then I'll have to go to lessons, but you won't, on account of you're new and they'll want to—"

"Hold on!" Mylanfyndra climbed out of bed and ran to the window. "Oh," she said, pointing. The girl was clad in leggings and tunic—made of gold! "What are those!"

Kori looked down. "These? My thermals, for skyrring, didn't you know? All athlynder-skyrr wear them—even Yoleyna under her ordinary clothes. She covers them so's to look ordinary—going about the towns, I don't suppose you noticed them? But the ones on active service—they don't cover up. This is their uniform, isn't it grand? You should see them pass overhead, so fast they streak with light."

Mylanfyndra looked to the girl's bare throat. "Where's your thruyl?"

Kori looked blankly. "Thruyl? Oh, we don't get those for years and years. Not until we have finished our schooling!"

A bell chimed across the courtyard, big, deep, melodious.

"There, didn't I say it would go at any moment, and we with scarcely time to talk!" Kori made a face. "Will you sit with me at noon break? See you then," she cried, then vanished through the bushes in a flash of gold, not waiting for answer.

Mylanfyndra watched her go, frowning.

. . . *we don't get those for years and years* . . .

She fetched her thruyl and slipped it on.

Frown changed to scowl.

194

I will not give it up, I will not! she told herself, fiercely. On a thought, she quickly made her bed, and hid the thruyl under the pillow.

There came a light tap on the outer door, and Yoleyna entered with a large ewer of hot water and a bunch of clothes over one arm. "So you are awake. What about you, Brevalan?"

At the mention of his name, Brevan emerged, looking tousled, but rested.

"Good morning," Yoleyna went on. "You're looking much better. Wash up, and I'll fetch breakfast—I'm joining you this time."

They washed quickly, dressed in their new clothes, the same for each; short tunic, and leggings loose-laced to the knee. Mylanfyndra felt strange out of skirts, but much more comfortable, she had to admit. Brevan laughed to see her, but she was in such good spirits this morning that she kicked up her feet, cutting a caper all around the sitting room. Not to be left out, Brevan joined in, hopping about on one foot with his hands in the air.

"Mercy," Yoleyna cried, bringing in the tray. "I see the air's quite gone to your heads!"

They ate porridge and pancakes and drank sweet, hot tea.

"When we have finished," Yoleyna said, "I'll take you to meet with the other Counselors."

"Counselors?" Mylanfyndra thought of the Elders in the Moot. She pictured herself and Brevan standing before a high table, the Counselors peering down over their noses.

"Don't look so worried, my dear. You have met us

already: Wurthen, and Althya, and Eothelwyn—and me. It will be no ordeal—at least, I hope not."

"Why?" Mylanfyndra was instantly on her mettle. "Why should it be?"

Yoleyna heaved a sigh. "It is time to surrender the thruyl."

"No!"

"I'm afraid so," Yoleyna said. "There can be no gainsaying it."

"I shall not give it up," Mylanfyndra declared stubbornly.

"You are forgetting," Yoleyna said gently. "It is not yours to keep. Please, fetch it out, Mylanfyndra."

Stiff-faced, Mylanfyndra retrieved fremma and thruyl and laid them on the table in front of Yoleyna as smartly as she dared.

"Nay," Yoleyna said. "You bring them. It's you who must give them up."

Yoleyna conducted them around the coom, down endless passages, through long narrow chambers, around to the front entrance hall, where the other three Counselors stood waiting.

"Ah," Wurthen said. "I trust you slept comfortably?"

"Yes, thank you, sir," Brevan said. Mylanfyndra said nothing, but stood, the fremma clutched in her hands.

"Good. Please come this way." Wurthen led them through an open archway off the hall. Inside, Mylanfyndra stopped, gazing around in awe. The whitewashed walls were lined with colorful likenesses of men and women in shining, golden suits. At every throat, the thruyl aflame; at every belt, the fremma. Before each portrait was a pedestal, topped by a dome-shaped glass. Sealed within each dome was a fremma, its contents arranged around it.

"Our honor gallery," Wurthen explained. "Those who died in the field."

Mylanfyndra moved down the room beside Brevan, looking from side to side. Suddenly, Brevan stopped, clutching at her sleeve. "Oh, Myl."

At the right, a young woman: hair blowing sideways, a stray wisp crossing her face. Mylanfyndra could scarcely breathe. After a moment, she opened the fremma, took out the horm and looked from the golden profile to the rich, full portrait.

"It's you, Myl. *You,*" Brevan whispered.

Mylanfyndra shook her head. "I don't look like that." Her nose was fat and her cheeks were pudgy.

"Not yet," Althya said. "But you will. When Breia was your age, she looked almost exactly like you, Mylanfyndra."

Mylanfyndra gazed up. "I'm not tall, and my hair is squitty."

"Who said Breia was tall?" Althya said. "As for her hair, yours is much the same color, and as thick."

"Hers is so long."

"You can grow yours long, if you want."

Mylanfyndra's gaze dropped from the portrait to the pedestal beneath. The dome was empty. She looked at the fremma, felt its weight on her palm. Without a word, she held it out.

"Thank you, Mylanfyndra." Wurthen took the fremma, shook it out. "These are yours, I think," he said, holding out the baby tags. "Well, don't you want them?" he prompted, when they made no move to take them.

"Oh, yes," Brevan said. He pulled his and wrapped it spirally around his finger.

"Perhaps," Yoleyna said, holding her hands out and taking them, "we could have them fashioned properly into rings, Wurthen?"

"Yes, yes! What a grand idea!" To Mylanfyndra's surprise, Wurthen handed thruyl, horm, and medron to her, the fremma to Brevan. Then he raised the dome lid, and directed Brevan how to place the pouch on the pedestal top. One by one, Mylanfyndra herself arranged the precious, golden treasures carefully around the pouch, then Wurthen replaced the dome, sealing in the whole. At the sight of those things lying there, Mylanfyndra felt quite bereft.

"Breialynda would be so proud of you this day," Wurthen declared. "That by some miracle you saved these priceless things, and brought them home."

Mylanfyndra shifted her feet. "Begging your pardon," she said, "but they saved us. If it weren't for them, we wouldn't be here." All at once, happiness expanded inside her like a hot drink in an empty stomach. She glanced to the next portrait. A man smiled down at her: long thin face, long nose, sleek dark hair, a dusting of gray at the temples; gray eyes alert. Looked strangely familiar, somehow . . . "Brevan!" She turned excitedly to Wurthen. "Please, who is that?"

"Who would you say, Mylanfyndra?"

Brevan was staring up at the portrait, his face a blank.

Mylanfyndra swallowed. "Our father?"

Brevan let go her hand.

Wurthen nodded. "You have gone to the heart of it, Mylanfyndra. As Breia was athlynder-skyrr, so was your father, Mahrulan."

Father! Mylanfyndra scanned the portrait, looking from it to Brevan and back again. The eyes, the nose: so like, she thought. Could he not see it?

Eothelwyn spoke. "Mahrulan was killed two years ago on a mission in the southern hemisphere. He never got over his loss. He and Breia were so close—they grew up together here. And he adored his two babies."

Mylanfyndra looked down. All those years on the mesa with Gven. Their father had grieved for them, and they giving him scarcely a thought.

"Mahrulan." Brevan moved up for a closer look. "What was he like?"

"Like you, Brevalan," Eothelwyn said. "Exactly. I recall him well at your age. You could be young Mahru standing there."

Brevan peered through the dome, eyeing their father's things.

Mylanfyndra remembered the garden, the statue marking their founder's grave. Didn't Yoleyna say athlynder-skyrr were buried there? "When our father died, did you bring him home?"

Wurthen nodded. "Indeed. Mahrulan lies in the garth with his fellows. Come, we will show you his grave."

It was nothing grand, just a simple rectangle marked with small, round rocks in a row of others. "I only wish your mother lay beside him, but . . ." His voice trailed off.

"Gven would have buried her." Mylanfyndra crouched,

passing her hand over the bossy stones. Grandpa would not have left Breia out to ash in the glair. Still, they might never find her grave. Secretly, she decided she was glad that Gven and Breia kept each other company up in the pod-lithra.

"It's time, Counselor," Althya said.

"So soon?" Wurthen smiled down at the children. "They're dragging you off to school already. Alas, poor me, to lose you so fast. Well, I assure you, we shall meet again before too long. But before you go, I have something to tell you:

"To you, the first athlynder-skyrr to be born to sky folk, I hereby decree that when you have finished your schooling, your parents' fremmas shall be handed down to you for use in the field—they would have wished it."

CHAPTER 24

"Now are you happy?" Brevan demanded, as Wurthen walked away with Althya and Eothelwyn.

"Of course she is," Yoleyna said. "And she will be even happier to start her lessons, as will you be also, young man."

Brevan snorted. "What's to learn? We flew here, didn't we?"

"That you did, and much credit to you. But there's much more to skyrring than that. Remember when Calen had you in the alley?"

"The whirlwind!" Mylanfyndra cried. Yoleyna ramming Calen, her body a fast, explosive blur but inches from the ground! "How did you do that?"

"By revolving upon my own axis, while thrusting forward at an angle. It is a much advanced figure, but one day you'll learn it," Yoleyna said, looking pleased that Mylanfyndra remembered.

"How long before we finish learning to skyrr and qualify?" Brevan said.

"Sorry to say it's still not that simple, young man. You'll need more than skyrring to be a sky messenger."

"Oh?"

"You must learn the skyways and starmaps. And how to use the thruyl."

"How to use it?" Brevan looked puzzled. "Don't you simply put it on and warm it up?"

Yoleyna shook her head. "If you had known how to use it, you could have signaled who you were and where you were exactly. By the time you have earned your thruyl, you'll be able to make it talk, in a manner of speaking."

"Oh," said Mylanfyndra, thinking how Wurthen had not seemed so surprised to see them. "Did you tell them we were coming?"

"In a manner of speaking." Yoleyna nodded.

"Now is that it?" Brevan demanded impatiently.

"Oh, no, Brevan. There's much more besides. You must master the world's many different languages—"

"But don't we all speak the same one?" Mylanfyndra thought of the folk they had met.

Yoleyna shook her head. "We are presently speaking a version of the Common Vernacular—the one you appear to have. But that will not get you far around Pyra. In addition—"

"Pyra?" the children said together.

Yoleyna threw up her hands. "What we call this world

we live in. I'm getting way ahead of myself, I see."

Pyra. Mylanfyndra repeated the word silently. These people gave everything a special name, it seemed. The mesa belt was the Gansor; the frontier town was Ludder's End; the orchard village was Ulfrond; and this home of athlynderskyrr was Falath-coom. Back in their old home, the mesa was simply the mesa; the town, the town. All these names had meanings, too. "Does Pyra have a special meaning, Yoleyna?"

The woman sighed. "Oh, dear. I might have known I'd not get off so pat." She subsided onto a nearby bench, motioned the children to sit on either side of her. "Pyra means 'egg.' "

"*Egg!*" Mylanfyndra stared.

"Why?" Brevan demanded. "It doesn't make sense."

"But it does," Yoleyna said. She bent down with a grunt, and, taking up a twig, she drew an oval in the dirt. "You see, the world is shaped like a giant egg—"

"Looks flat enough to me," Brevan declared.

"The egg is divided around the middle by a band of rock-studded clay."

"The Gansor!" Mylanfyndra cried. The studded belt.

Yoleyna nodded. "Why and how the mesas came to be you'll learn later on. All I'll tell you now is that the top half of Pyra—the one we're on—is called Telfyra. The southern half is called An-telfyra."

"Do people live down there, too?" Brevan asked.

"Aye, that they do."

"But they can't cross the Gansor!" Mylanfyndra cried. "Only athlynder-skyrr can do that!"

Yoleyna's eyes lit up. "There you have it, child. Now you really see why skyfolk are so vital to the world. We are the only link connecting north and south."

Brevan whistled. "No wonder the northern Houses laid siege," he said. "When do we learn more of this?"

Yoleyna stood and brushed down her skirt. "As soon as we get you into school," she said, smiling.

"*Then* will we be done?" Brevan persisted.

"Goodness, no." The woman laughed outright. "There's also reading, and writing, and numbers. Later, when you specialize, if you choose to be a Courier-Diplomat, there are the rules of law and protocol. Or, if you would be Loremaster, you must know by heart the Annals of the Realms, together with the Pyran Chronicles of Myth and Mystery. Or, if you'd be Pathfinder—"

"Pathfinder!" That had been Yoleyna's calling, if Kori told right. "What do they do?" Mylanfyndra said.

"They skyrr the unexplored regions, seeking remote peoples, like the folk on your mesa. It can be perilous work, but it is most rewarding."

"What do you do when you've found them?" Brevan said.

"We teach them of the outer world, and learn of theirs," Yoleyna said. "We expand their choices, they enrich our Chronicles."

Mylanfyndra couldn't imagine how the townsfolk could enrich anything. "Will Pathfinders seek the mesa, Yoleyna?"

"I should hope so," Brevan cried. "Teach them a lesson; make them pay."

Yoleyna shook her head. "It's not like that. We don't

punish folk; we don't *make* them do anything."

"But they think us evil, they believe in the wyrth, and Koos and Anlahr. You have to stop them, make them see, teach them what's right to believe!"

"Brevan, Brevan." Yoleyna folded her arms. "That's not what we're about! Look—there are so many *right* beliefs around Pyra. So many different folks, all with their own myths and laws. Who's to say that one system is better than the rest, and that others must give up theirs to follow it?"

"But what if those beliefs nearly get you killed, Yoleyna?"

"We have judges and keepers of the peace to deal with that contingency. Resolving strife is outside our sphere, Brevan. Remember our sky symbol on the horm? The lightning from the heels speaks the speed of the messenger. The lightning from the hands signifies the knowledge we carry from land to land. Enlightenment is our brief. To spread the world's mosaic of thought, to uphold its variety. We sky folk believe the world would be a sorry place if everyone was the same."

Brevan held up his hands. "My head is spilling over," he said.

"When will the Pathfinders go to seek the mesa?" Mylanfyndra said.

"Not until after the glair, of course."

"What will they do, exactly?"

"Land secretly and observe, for a start. Think of the shock to see strangers from another place—when they believe the mesa is all there is."

"You must warn whoever," Mylanfyndra said. "The townsfolk will be afraid. They will think the Pathfinders evil. Perhaps the ones who infected us. They might even try to kill whoever—and think themselves in the right."

"Thanks for the warning, Mylanfyndra," Yoleyna said. She turned toward the rear wing door. "We're hoping to learn much from you of your mesa, so that we can avoid mistakes. Meanwhile, the children are in the mess hall. Are you ready to join them?"

Mylanfyndra's stomach did a bit of skyrring on its own, until she remembered Kori. Yoleyna led them through the doorway, steered them left to the schoolhouse quarter, and delivered them into the care of Valen and Cia, masters in skyrring, who were presiding over the noon meal. "Good luck," she said. "I'll see you at suppertime."

The meal was noisy—and more fun than Mylanfyndra had known in so long. Everybody talked at once, everybody asked questions, then answered them before she and Brevan had chance. And the feats she and Brevan were supposed to have accomplished! Almost they might be Koos and Anlahr themselves!

Kori nagged Mylanfyndra to take the empty dormitory cot next to hers.

"My cover's red; yours is blue—unless you'd like to ex-change," she said. "You will choose me, won't you? Oh, I can't wait for tonight." She leaned over, whispered in Mylanfyndra's ear. "After they put out the lights, we can talk if you'll whisper. Tell me how you rode the firestorms? And I'll tell you—oh, compared to you, I haven't much to say at all!"

When the meal was over, Brevan and Mylanfyndra received their practice thermals, and a pair of feather-light golden boots that fitted over the leggings. Then Valen and Cia took the class out over Lake Falath, a water so vast Mylanfyndra could not see its farther shores. She soared, found the suit comfortable up in the high currents, and allowing much more freedom than clumsy skirts. Warming to the exercise, she wheeled and glided, exulting in the feel of air slipping clean around her body. She was halfway through a banking turn when a treacherous downdraft caught her and nearly dumped her into the lake.

"That is the lake effect," Cia explained, diving to catch her. "When you have all mastered great Falath's tricks, then you may travel anywhere!"

But she already had, thought Mylanfyndra. Abashed, she rose to rejoin the class.

"You recovered well," Kori called, as they moved into another maneuver. "Most of us crashed worse than that. You must've been skyrring a long time."

During the course of the afternoon, Mylanfyndra saw how closely the others watched her and Brevan, assessing their every move, and wondered nervously how long the noontime's praises would last. But, to her relief, as the lesson progressed, she found herself and Brevan well respected, and better, by the end of the day, Brevan was firm friends with Qendo, a rangy An-telfyran boy a year his senior; Mylanfyndra, with Kori. When they returned to the coom, Mylanfyndra felt foolish at the idea of going to the guest chambers. After a hurried consultation, she and Brevan sent a message to Yoleyna that they were ready to move in with the rest.

Besides the dormitories, there was a large and comfortable common room, filled with board and counter games, and books for those who had learned to read. Kori showed Mylanfyndra how to play Skyrr-the-Gansor, where one threw dice to get from Telfyra at one end of the board to An-telfyra at the other while avoiding the many perils between. Brevan sat with Qendo and a group of other boys, expanding with wide gestures on his adventures in the charnon.

A good day, Mylanfyndra thought, as she lay in her cot thinking of Breia and Mahrulan. A wonderful, exhilarating day, skyrring high over the lake, breathing in the cold, clean air. She thought of Ebbwe, shut underground. She could still see the girl's face pressed against the cage bars that last afternoon. Ebbwe had freed them, now Ebbwe was the prisoner.

Mylanfyndra turned over on her back, staring up into the dark. She did not know, she had not asked: when the Pathfinders found the mesa, could folk leave it, if they wanted to?

The next day, Cia took the children to Eothelwyn's Chamber of Records, where he and Althya waited. "We shall meet, all together, for one hour a day," Althya said. "You shall teach us about your mesa, and we in return will teach you about Pyra."

"Where's Yoleyna?" Mylanfyndra said, at the same time looking all around the high, wide chamber lined with scroll-filled shelves.

"She was called out on a mission," Eothelwyn said. "She'll be gone for several days." He gestured them to sit at a large table in the center of the room. On it were scrolls of parchment and writing materials; a pot of blue ink and several quills.

For the next hour, Althya asked about the mesa. First, the climate: the year's quarters, and eight seasons. As Mylanfyndra told, Brevan took quill and scroll, and, under Eothelwyn's direction, drew the year's wheel, showing the length of each season, just as it was on the Moot Hall wall.

In return, Eothelwyn showed the children how the mesa belt had formed. How the clay had eroded over many ages, leaving the plugs of rock behind.

"As you saw, most of the mesas are red," Eothelwyn said. "Being made of larval rock." He told of great fires raging, and metal spouting, and stone boiling in the beginning of the world.

At the end of the hour, Eothelwyn sat back. "That is good," he said. "We are all learning much. I, for one, look forward to tomorrow."

Brevan took up his quill and twirled it about. "I liked using this thing. Will I work with it again?"

"Every day." Eothelwyn smiled. "You have a good hand, Brevalan."

"And you speak well, Mylanfyndra," Althya said. "It is a pleasure to work with you."

Mylanfyndra flushed. "Thank you," she said.

Brevan hung back. "I want to make maps and pictures like yours," he said, gazing down on Eothelwyn's handiwork.

"You shall," the Recorder said, smiling. "I shall teach you myself."

At the door, Mylanfyndra paused. "When the mesa folk know about the outside world," she began, picking her words with care. "If one wanted to leave, would it be possible?"

Althya looked into Mylanfyndra's eyes, and it seemed to Mylanfyndra that the woman knew exactly what was on her mind. "Why, yes. We'd carry them."

"But," Mylanfyndra went on, remembering what Yoleyna had said about not interfering. "What if other folk—those who made the rules—didn't want that person to leave?"

"We would consider the merits of the case," Althya said. "Try to do what was best for all concerned. Why, have you someone in mind?"

Mylanfyndra told of Ebbwe, how their friend had saved their lives. How she was stuck back there. Words spilled out, how Ebbwe was geth, the lowest of the low. "I bet they wouldn't let her leave. She's too useful, even if they call her the dregs!" Mylanfyndra cried. "But she doesn't belong there. She deserves a better life."

"I see." Althya nodded. "Well, there is a rule, a protocol. It is the Law of Sanctuary, whereby folk ask for the Freedom of the Lands. But there are strict conditions for its application."

Mylanfyndra clasped her hands tightly. "What are they?"

"First, the candidate must personally ask for sanctuary. Second, he or she must not be seeking to avoid some penalty for breach of law, or to create by their leaving hardship on those left behind. And, if the person is a child, the parents must consent to the departure."

Mylanfyndra clasped her hands. "Ebbwe fits! She fits! She

wants to leave! She dreams of a place like Telfyra. And as for hardship—no one would miss her—and she's an orphan with no one to care if she lives or dies!" She looked to Althya. "When the Pathfinder goes to seek the mesa, could Brevan and I go, too, as guides?"

"*You?*" Althya took Mylanfyndra's hand. "I think we'd better sit down. Now," Althya said, when they were seated. "This is no small request, Mylanfyndra. While we do not coddle our young, we do not send them out into the active field."

"But we came from that place!" Mylanfyndra cried. "Please—*please,* I beg of you, let us go with whoever, we must!" She pointed to the table. "Those maps, aren't we helping to make them?"

Althya sighed. "You know what I mean, Mylanfyndra. 'Tis a miracle you came out of there alive. Why, your own mother—" She broke off.

"That was the glair," Mylanfyndra urged. "When we go, it will be over. You talk about your ways," she went on, as Althya looked unbending. "But you also say you respect differences. Brevan and I are different from the other students here. That no one can deny."

Althya looked startled. Then "That's right enough," she said, with a gleam in her eyes. "When Yoleyna comes back, we will speak of what you ask. But I make no promises, understand? Meanwhile, work hard and learn your lessons—one of which is patience." Smiling now, Althya walked Mylanfyndra to the door where Brevan still waited.

"What was all *that* about?" Brevan said, as they made their way back to class. "Not another fuss, I hope?"

Mylanfyndra explained. "If they let us go, will you come?"

Brevan frowned. "Of course, Myl. We owe Ebbwe. But I doubt they'll let us."

Yoleyna returned to the coom, but several days passed and Mylanfyndra had no sign of her. Mylanfyndra waited patiently as Althya had bidden, but each day she and Brevan went to the Record Chamber, there was no mention of her request. "Don't pester," Brevan warned. "You'll only rile them and then they'll say no just because."

Mylanfyndra shook her head. "They're not like that," she said. But she did heed Brevan's caution, and bided her time as calmly as she could.

About ten days after Yoleyna's return, the children were summoned to meet with Wurthen and the rest.

"You say you want to find your friend, and bring her to Telfyra?" Wurthen looked solemn. "This is a most generous thought, Mylanfyndra. But have you any idea of the responsibility we feel toward you and Brevan? Can you imagine how we'd be should anything happen to you now?"

The words bubbled in Mylanfyndra's throat. All about how she didn't care, how she had to find Ebbwe, how they owed her. "Yes, sir," she said.

"And you have already learned how difficult it will be to find your mesa. Tell me, Mylanfyndra, how many mesas are said to be in the Gansor—in the known areas alone?"

"Over five thousand, sir." Mylanfyndra looked him squarely in the eye. "But our mesa's no more than one day and night into the gray region, maybe much less."

"How do you mean?"

"I traveled for one day and one night without seeing anything but mist, sir. I could have been skyrring over red mesas all the time."

"Or gray ones, or a mixture of the two. See how hopeless this is, Mylanfyndra?" Wurthen sighed, and shifted in his seat. "You see, even if you were on the *very* edge, finding your mesa would be no easy matter. The Gansor is many miles wide. And the gray boundaries are ill-defined in places. Sometimes the change from gray to red is quick. Sometimes the red mesas and the gray mesas are all mixed in together for miles. That leaves a lot of territory to cover, my dear."

"We're working with Eothelwyn to narrow it down."

"So far with no success."

"No, sir." Mylanfyndra's voice was barely a whisper.

Wurthen sighed again. "Until we pinpoint your zone within the greater region, it's useless to discuss whether you may go or no."

Mylanfyndra leaned forward. "But when we do, sir—could we—would you let us go then?"

Wurthen smiled. "You are most persistent, young lady. Let us say this: find the way to your mesa, and we'll talk again."

CHAPTER 25

Days passed, weeks. The children settled down, made progress. The strangeness of having friends, of being with others besides themselves, wore off, and they grew used not only to sleeping apart, but also to going out and doing things singly. Brevan seemed to have put the mesa quite behind him, Mylanfyndra thought, watching her brother skyrring, and laboring at his letters and numbers. He was so caught up these days in his activities that he spoke of it only in the sessions with Althya and Eothelwyn. One day, as she walked in the garden, Brevan came running out to find her. "Myl, Myl! Guess what!" Valen was taking a mapping group around the lake on a month-long trip and there was one space left. "Qendo is in it, and he's asked me to go with him. Should I, do you think?"

It was all over his face. He wanted to go so badly. Map-making was turning out to be Brevan's favorite subject, and this was a wonderful chance to work in the field. But he clearly felt awkward going without her.

Mylanfyndra was touched. "What if I said no?"

He looked disconcerted. "Well, I—"

Mylanfyndra threw her arms around him. "Of course you must go, silly! I think it's wonderful that you have a place, being so new."

He returned the squeeze, looking vastly relieved. "You're sure you don't mind, Myl? I feel bad, leaving you."

"What if it were the other way around? What if I wanted to go off and do something without you?"

He frowned. "I'd make you go, Myl."

"So there's your answer!"

He ran off to tell the news and to make ready, for they were setting out at dawn the next day. Mylanfyndra watched him go, thinking how wonderful it would have been had they both been leaving to fetch Ebbwe from the mesa. But she began to suspect that even if they could go, Brevan would be reluctant now to leave Qendo and the other fellows behind.

As for Mylanfyndra, good a friend as Kori was, there were things she might never share with the girl, so she still had some reserve. Lately, when things lay on her mind, she took to visiting Mahrulan's grave, to confide in him as she had in Gven.

"I don't know," she said, sitting herself down beside the stones. "Brevan's gotten so caught in things here—as he should have," she added hastily. "I'm loving it here,

215

too. Everyone is so nice, I wouldn't want to be anyplace else. But I can't seem to get on with things with Ebbwe stuck back there in utter *misery*. I wish I knew what to do."

She gazed around at the bright garden, at the colors and shapes of everything, trying to see them with Ebbwe's eyes, and right then she hit on an idea. Eothelwyn and Althya were still recording the most important facts about the mesa, such customs and laws. While all this would prove useful for observing the mesa, Mylanfyndra couldn't see how it would help to find it.

What if there were clues on the mesa as to its whereabouts? Nothing big, for they'd covered all that. Mylanfyndra thought of the common things of everyday. Shells, 'lithworms. They wouldn't get to those for a time. But suppose she made actual pictures of them which could be seen in an instant?

She jumped and ran inside. "I need to draw," she said to Cia. "Can you give me things to use?"

"To draw? Of course." Cia found her a stack of empty scrolls, and a box of brightly colored inks. Mylanfyndra set to work. For the next few days, she sat every spare minute, meticulously drawing each thing she could think of on the mesa. She started with the lowly stoneflowers, and weeds and grasses. Then she drew 'lithworms, and 'lith rats, and other small animals that burrowed in the doft. After that, she started on the birds, beginning with the tiny doftdauber, through the firebird, all the way up to the great cutwing. As the pictures piled up, she took them to Eothelwyn and Althya. The counselors praised the pictures highly. "Look at this cutwing," Althya said. "It is much like ours, except for the dark stripe on the head."

"These will be so useful, Mylanfyndra," Eothelwyn said. He brought from the shelves sheaves of drawings done in other lands, to augment the charts.

"Truly, you never cease to surprise us," Althya said. "The way you go and do the very right thing without ever being told!" Althya sifted through Mylanfyndra's latest sketches, then, exclaiming, held one up. "What is this?"

Mylanfyndra leaned over. "A firebird."

"Firebird!" Althya handed the drawing to Eothelwyn, who examined it minutely. "A hetzan, you do agree?"

Eothelwyn nodded, his eyes gleaming.

Mylanfyndra felt a spark of excitement. The firebird clearly meant something to them.

"Tell us about it," Eothelwyn said.

Mylanfyndra told everything she knew. "Gven looked for their shelter, but he never found it. Of course he wouldn't, for they, like all the other birds, must fly off the mesa entirely," she finished.

"Indeed they do," Althya said. "But where we also have your other birds, and would not notice seasonal additions"—she pointed to the drawing of the cutwing—"this one is not native to either north or south. We call it *hetzan,* which means flamewing. At the height of summer, when the firestorms hit the Gansor, these birds appear in great numbers on both Telfyra and An-telfyra. No one has sought to discover whence they come, or whither they return when the storms are done. But knowing they come from your mesa . . ."

Althya and Eothelwyn conferred in low tones.

"Mylanfyndra," Althya said at last. "We must go to speak with Wurthen. Go back to your quarters, and we will send for you later."

"Why?" Mylanfyndra asked, her excitement rising. "Is it to do with finding the mesa?"

Althya smiled. "Maybe."

For two whole days, Mylanfyndra waited for a summons. She could scarcely eat or sleep, and she could not think of work. On the third day, she was just off skyrring, when Wurthen summoned her.

"You still want to find your friend, Mylanfyndra?" the Counselor said.

"Yes." Mylanfyndra looked to the four counselors assembled, trying to guess their thought.

Wurthen nodded. "You know there has been small chance, Mylanfyndra. Until two days ago."

Mylanfyndra drew in breath. "You mean—you found the mesa?"

"No," Yoleyna said. "You did."

"I?"

"Your drawing of the hetzan has helped us locate its general area," Eothelwyn said. "Now we know that the hetzan is from your mesa, that the flock splits, one half heading north, the other, south. Given their rate of flight, and the distance in days—which we got from you—we have guessed their dual paths and traced them backward. Where they cross, that indicates their probable zone of origin—a fairly wide one, I'm afraid. But it's a start."

Mylanfyndra looked around again. She couldn't exactly follow all that Eothelwyn was saying, but everyone certainly looked pleased with her. She turned to Wurthen, pressing her advantage. "What you promised . . ."

"I doubt there's a Pathfinder who would take you *officially*," Wurthen said. "But—" He looked to Yoleyna and gave a nod.

The Seeker sat up. "When I was a girl like you," she said, "someone like Ebbwe saved my life, too. Like you, I begged my tutor to let me seek that person and bring her to Telfyra. Do you know, he took me himself—of course, that place wasn't so far off the beaten track," she added hastily.

"Did you find the person?"

"Oh, yes. In fact, she lives in Ulfrond. You met her on the way here."

"Fusci!" Mylanfyndra could see the woman now, smiling and waving up at them. "Who was your tutor, Yoleyna?"

Yoleyna ducked her head in Wurthen's direction. "Our head counselor was teaching star charts then." She climbed heavily back onto her feet. "Now it is my turn. It is a while since I went out a Pathfinder, but I've not lost my skills, I should hope. Althya, I thank you for your offer to go with us, but if I need assistance, I shall signal. Mylanfyndra, everything is ready. You shall go to bed early in the guest chambers. We leave before sunup."

"But Brevan," Mylanfyndra began, then nodded. "He can meet her here," she said, and knew that it would be well.

CHAPTER 26

An hour before sunrise, Mylanfyndra and Yoleyna headed south in a strong tailwind, bearing packs so light Mylanfyndra could scarcely feel hers. On Yoleyna's advice, she wore her old mesa clothes over her thermals, just in case, the Seeker said. But what a difference the thermals made, she thought, remembering the cold of the coomward journey. No wonder Yoleyna had seemed comfortable, wearing those wonderful things under her street clothes!

In her backpack was a spare suit for Ebbwe, and an extra bedroll.

Ebbwe! Her stomach did a roll. "I was thinking, Yoleyna," she called. "About Fusci being lonely now. Would she take Ebbwe in, do you suppose?"

"It crosses my mind."

"Ebbwe could work in the orchards, maybe."

"Sounds possible," Yoleyna said.

In two days they reached the Edge, riding high above Jag's mining camp a little after dusk. Then Telfyra was left behind, and they were riding a southerly current out into the Gansor. All night, they rode that skyway; when the sun came up, the red path of mesas stretched before them, as far as they could see. Overhead, the sky was once again its normal blue, and the only gold was the sun. As Mylanfyndra flew, she felt the many crosscurrents whoofing against her face, and each time, she wanted to ask "Is this the one?" But she knew it was too soon. She herself had traveled on for at least eight hours after joining the northern skyway. Sure enough, Yoleyna continued south, until, about midday, she slowed and cast about. "Ah," she said, pointing west. "This will be your current, I think."

As they turned off the main skyroad and headed into the westerly wind, Mylanfyndra felt the air slacken. Definitely a side road, she thought, realizing how well she now could gauge the airs. "This wind was much stronger before," she remarked. "And hotter—but that was during the glair."

For three days, they flew against the cold, high headwind. Even in its weakened state, the force of the wind was very tiring. At Yoleyna's insistence, they descended many times through the warmer layers to rest on a mesa and eat. Each night, the Pathfinder called a halt. She found them a sheltered spot to lie and had them sleep, lying comfortably on featherlight bedrolls of the golden stuff. As she fell asleep, Mylanfyndra thought of Ebbwe sleeping in the brug. "Not much longer," she whispered. What would her friend say to see her? she wondered in growing excitement. Dear

Ebbwe. She remembered her friend's small figure rushing across the hot cobbles, waving her arms. Shrieking as they hurtled toward the wyrthwall. Dashing into the Warren entrance. She pictured Ebbwe's face on seeing her. Of course, she'd cry out, then stifle the sound, looking about for Krels . . .

The nearer they drew to the gray region, the more often Ebbwe filled Mylanfyndra's thoughts, until she could scarcely keep them in.

On the third day, they spotted the first gray mesa.

"Hurrah! We're there!" Mylanfyndra cried.

"Perhaps," Yoleyna replied.

As they approached, they found it to be a chance gray plug surrounded by red ones. "I see what Wurthen meant about the boundary being irregular," Mylanfyndra said ruefully.

"Don't be discouraged," Yoleyna said. "It tells us that at least we're getting close to the gray region."

Sure enough, during the next hour or so, they found more gray mesas, and a number of red-and-gray ones also. The mixed ones increased until, there: stretching away, a veritable sea of gray surrounded by mists.

Mylanfyndra cried out excitedly. "Now are we almost there?"

Yoleyna laughed. "Well, we've found the general area, at least. But according to Eothelwyn's calculations, the zone where we'll find your mesa stretches for several hours north and south of here. Take my hand," she said. "We'll land and rest." They alighted on a bare, gray mesa, and sheltered in the lee of a long, low bank. As they ate and drank, Mylanfyndra thought again of Ebbwe and smiled.

"What are you thinking, Mylanfyndra?"

"I'm trying to guess what Ebbwe will do when she sees me. She'll certainly be surprised."

"Surprised?" Yoleyna sat up. "Shocked is more the word, I think. Surely she must think you dead."

Mylanfyndra's smile cut. "Oh. I hadn't thought of that."

They napped for a while. When they awoke, Yoleyna consulted Eothelwyn's charts. She set her finger on a tangled line which separated red from gray. 'We are here, and this is where we must search." She slid her finger up and down. Mylanfyndra nodded, thinking how quick it looked on the map, until one realized that a finger's width covered a space as big as Lake Falath!

They rose and began to edge northward, circling over the search area until midafternoon, finding nothing. Sometimes, gray mesas gave place abruptly to red ones for a whole stretch at a time; sometimes, red and gray were mingled in together, like colored rocks thrown by a monstrous hand. The sun was near the horizon, when Yoleyna called a halt. As they looked for the best place to land, Mylanfyndra called out.

"Yoleyna, look!"

High above, tiny black dots, moving in a straggly line. "The firebirds! They're returning to the mesa!"

"Let us hope," Yoleyna said.

They tagged the birds for the best part of an hour. "They're a tattered lot," the Seeker observed, as she and Mylanfyndra drew closer. "Those wings don't look strong enough to carry them far."

"A good sign, don't you see?" Mylanfyndra cried triumphantly. "The birds are almost home. Soon after they land in the podlithra, they'll shed what's left of their wings. And they'll grow fat and waddly and squawky again—till next year!"

"Truly," Yoleyna said. "Your hetzans are strange as any—oho, they're circling, Mylanfyndra."

They dove toward the birds and the clustered mesas below them—and there! "That one!" cried Mylanfyndra. "See the one they're headed for? I can just make out the Chute! And the Warren—and yonder, the town!"

The birds spiraled down.

"It's all gray," Yoleyna remarked, following after. "The trees—no, I mean podliths of course, and the houses—they all merge into the clay. Save for those hetzans we might have spent days spotting this place."

As they went lower, the mist swirled up to engulf them. For a moment, Mylanfyndra's heart jumped. Only mist, she reminded herself. That's all. A moment later, covered in droplets, they broke through, then passed the cliffs, to hover over the Warren, just as the sun went down.

"We'll avoid the town, Mylanfyndra, and find somewhere to rest until it's quite dark. Lead the way."

Mylanfyndra circled up into the podlithra, over many burnt-out spots. "The glair was bad this year. See," she said, pointing. "There's Gven's hut. It's quite destroyed." And no sign of rebuilding.

"This is just terrible, my dear," Yoleyna said, turning slowly, looking down. "No one, either north or south, has ever seen such devastation. I well see why your Anlahr! What resourceful minds, to find some sense in all this! Your mesa spirits may offer the greatest myths of all time!"

"Even though they're not true?"

Yoleyna smiled. "Myth is quite another way of telling truth than fact, Mylanfyndra. This you will learn later on, when you study the book of Pyran myths." She moved lower, shaking her head. "Why, the fire has not only burned the stone, but it has crushed it in places—look, those podliths have exploded into dust!"

They moved slowly along to Gven's knoll, Yoleyna stopping many times on the way to exclaim and shake her head. Perhaps, thought Mylanfyndra, the mesa was special after all, for its very awfulness!

Mylanfyndra found the knoll untouched, glad to say. She led the way down, and ran to Gven's bole. "This is where we buried Grandpa," she said, stroking the stone.

"It is very fine," Yoleyna said, coming up to see. "He was a lucky man to have had such fine children as you to lay him to rest. I for one would not be averse to lying here beneath the stars." She walked slowly to the hill's crown and gazed all around. "Breialynda . . ." she murmured, and turned to Mylanfyndra. "Do you think she could be buried somewhere near?"

Mylanfyndra looked doubtfully around the high hilltop. "Gven found the three of us on his way down to the Warren. Yet he could have been up here," she added quickly. "This was his favorite place, and, as you said, the first firestorm struck early that year, taking everyone by surprise."

"Mmmmm." Yoleyna shot Mylanfyndra a wise look. "You think it unlikely, eh? Still, we both agree it's a nice thought. Very well, let us sit in this place and take a bite, remembering Gven and your mother."

They sat and silently helped themselves to waybread. "How long before it's safe to go down, Mylanfyndra?" Yoleyna said presently.

"About an hour. It's best to get there whilst they're having supper. We'll wait behind the women's bathhouse, and catch Ebbwe on her way to wash."

When it was time, they rose and made their way over the dark rooftops, via the marketplace. In the center, a heap of twisted metal lay fused to the ground: the remains of the thieves cage.

"You poor children," Yoleyna murmured. "When I think what could have happened! Thank goodness you got out in time!"

"Nay, thank Ebbwe," Mylanfyndra said.

They passed over the squat bulk of the Moot Hall, and the laundry with its heat-filled chimneys, and headed for the warehouse quarter. Everything looked so bare and bleak to Mylanfyndra, much worse than before.

As she neared the brug, the old smells hit, filling her with dread. Yoleyna took her hand. "The fear won't quit for quite a while, maybe never. But we'll teach you how to put it to good use."

They alighted behind the brug, and peered through a rear window. Ebbwe was lying on her pile, eyes closed, her supper plate beside her—untouched? "There she is!" Mylanfyndra whispered, puzzled.

"She does not look well," Yoleyna whispered back.

"It's the light," Mylanfyndra said. "Ebbwe's never sick." So why was she lying like that?

A sudden, loud noise started them back.

"Mercy! What was that?" Yoleyna said.

"Krels, banging the pot. It's bathhouse time."

They retreated behind the women's shed, just as the first figures erupted from the brug door. Folk streamed to and fro, in and out, chattering noisily. "Don't worry," Mylanfyndra said. "She'll be last, you see."

But Ebbwe did not come.

"There's Fos," Mylanfyndra said. The familiar figure looked thinner, more stooped than ever. Mylanfyndra dodged out, called. Fos turned. For a moment, he stood, frozen, his mouth open. Then he spun about as though to bolt back into the brug.

"Fos! Fos!" Mylanfyndra urged in a low voice. "Don't go! It's really me and I need you!"

The boy halted uncertainly, then, glancing left and right, he moved to the corner of the shed, taking care to keep his distance. "Why aren't you dead? Where's your—?" He stepped back. "Who's that?"

"This is Yoleyna," Mylanfyndra said quickly. "Brevan's doing just fine, he's—Fos, there's no time to tell. Where's Ebbwe?"

He was still gaping. "Inside. She'll not be coming out."

"Not?"

"Leg's broke. Even Krels can't get her up."

A wave of fear rushed in. "Broken her leg? How?"

Fos shrugged. "Laundry, I think. Slipped. Got herself home, and passed out. That were three days since."

Yoleyna took Mylanfyndra's arm. "Can we fetch her out, my dear?"

Mylanfyndra shook her head. "They'll have stopped up the hole."

"That one, maybe." Fos dug his toe in the dirt. "But not the other."

"Other?"

Fos hesitated, looking from Mylanfyndra to Yoleyna. "Oh, what's the difference," he muttered. "She's a goner either way. It's in the back wall, just the same. Wait an hour, I'll show you," he said, then took off.

"Well, that's a start. We'll need something for splints; my shawl will do for bindings," Yoleyna said briskly.

"I'll find some 'lith stakes," Mylanfyndra said. *Ebbwe hurt!*

"Your friend, Fos, looks . . . in need. Would he want someone to fetch him? I could signal home."

"I don't know. He's a funny one." Mylanfyndra foraged around, found four good vine lengths. "Will these do?"

Yoleyna hefted one. "These are *solid!* No wonder you children are so tough. These are fine," she said, picking out a pair and discarding the rest.

Another banging, Krels calling for lights out.

The brug fell silent.

They moved out from behind the bathhouse to wait in the lee of the brug wall. Not for long. There came a faint scraping, a hole appeared in the base of the wall very close to Ebbwe's stake, and Fos emerged, head first.

"She made it a few weeks back," Fos said. "Just because. They beat her up bad in the Warren."

"For helping us?"

"They said the wyrth—" Fos broke off, staring at

Yoleyna. "They said you had to be dead in the glair."

"They were wrong," Mylanfyndra answered. "As you can see, I'm quite fine and having a wonderful time. Fos, would you like—"

"I'm sure you are," Fos cut in. "Well, there it is," he said, stepping back. "I'm off now. I told her you're here. Dunno if she heard."

"Fos, wait: do you want to come with us?" Mylanfyndra said.

"Where?" He glanced to Yoleyna. "You mean, down. . . ?"

"Oh, no, Fos!" Mylanfyndra grabbed his sleeve. "Nothing like that. See? I'm as solid as you are."

Fos shook free, then reached out and touched her face gingerly. "This place, where is it, then? Ain't nowhere else but the mesa."

"Oh, there is, Fos. It's . . . way over. It's wonderful. Full of feathers and shells. You'll love it. We can get someone to carry you right now if you want." For a moment, Mylanfyndra thought he'd say yes, but then he sighed, and shook his head.

"Thanks, but I stay here," he said, and crawled back through the hole.

"He doesn't trust us," Yoleyna observed.

"It's not that." Mylanfyndra explained about Harv and his Sending.

"Oh, I see," Yoleyna said. "Well, he'll maybe change his mind one day. Listen, my dear," she went on, bending to inspect the hole. "I cannot get through that. Slip off your backpack. You are going to have to fetch Ebbwe out by yourself."

"How, her with a broken leg?" Mylanfyndra dropped her pack to the ground.

"I don't know. But get her this far, and I'll do the rest."

Mylanfyndra ducked down, wriggled through the narrow gap.

Heat enfolded her like a sour blanket. Mylanfyndra paused, not daring to breathe. She stood, waited for the strangeness to pass, for the sense of the familiar to return: the sleeping shapes, the night noises. She thought of Vel and stiffened. Relax, she told herself. You're long gone . . .

Mylanfyndra eased her feet along the dozen or so steps to Ebbwe's place, then paused, marking where piles had been shifted. She moved on, easy, easy, along by the wall. Almost there. Suddenly, her heart began to race. She could almost feel Krels's eyes upon her. No, why should they be? she told herself sternly. She was not there anymore. Reaching Ebbwe's stake, she groped about, found her friend's shoulder. "Ebbwe?"

Fos spoke quietly in her ear. "She won't wake. She's fevered."

Mylanfyndra straightened, fighting despair. Gven all over again, except there was no Brevan and this dead weight fell to her alone. Oh, to have come all this way . . .

"Can you help hoist her over my shoulder, Fos?"

The boy glanced around. "Be quick," he said.

Between them, they lifted Ebbwe, carefully resting her legs against Mylanfyndra's front. Then Fos ducked off and disappeared.

Left alone, Mylanfyndra inched back toward the hole, testing each step carefully. Just a short way, she told herself, clenching her teeth. How could Ebbwe weigh so heavy, being so small? It felt as if her friend were pressing her into the ground. Still, she might be thankful for small advantages, Mylanfyndra thought, recalling the last time she had carried the girl, when that weight had also thrown itself about! Almost there: Mylanfyndra sagged with relief—a mistake. She stumbled, jerking Ebbwe's leg. Ebbwe moaned, people stirred. There came a sleepy cry. Quickly, Mylanfyndra lowered Ebbwe to the floor. "Yoleyna! Here!" She pushed Ebbwe into the hole, head first.

"I have her," Yoleyna called, and pulled the girl through. Mylanfyndra scrambled after to find Yoleyna poised for flight, Ebbwe in her arms.

"They're coming, Mylanfyndra. Get the sticks!"

Krels rounded the corner, lantern raised. He pulled up short.

"You!" He looked past Mylanfyndra. *"Toova?"* The lantern fell from his hand. As it hit the ground, Yoleyna and Mylanfyndra rose, leaving a mass of stunned faces behind.

"Head for the cliff," Yoleyna called. "We'll have time to fix the splint, I think."

"Will Ebbwe be all right?" Mylanfyndra touched her friend's head lightly, found the hair matted and stiff.

"She'll be fine," Yoleyna said. "Once the leg is spliced and the fever's down. We came just in time, though."

Mylanfyndra breathed out. "The leg will mend?"

"She'll be running around before you know it."

Mylanfyndra moved in closer. "Fusci will love Ebbwe, won't she?" she asked anxiously.

"Count on it," Yoleyna said, kicking forward. "Come on, let's get her home!"

Pronunciation Guide

a = cat, ā = late; e = met, ē = meet; i = pin, ī = pine; o
= mod, ō = mode; u = put, ū = loop; oo = look, $\overline{oo}$ =
cool; then = hard th, thin = soft th
Consonants hard, unless otherwise indicated

PROPER NAMES

Althya	al-*thee*-uh (soft th)
Anlahr	*an*-lah
Antelfyra	*an*-tel-*feer*-uh (second accent slighter than first)
Aothelwyn	ā-ō-*thel*-win (soft th)
Breialynda	brī-uh-*lin*-duh
Brevalan	*brev*-uh-lan
Brevan	*brev*-n
Calen	*kā*-len
Cia	*see*-yuh
Daven-Elder	*da*-ven-*el*-der
Ebbwe	*eb*-way
Falath-byr	*fa*-lath-*beer*
Falath-coom	*fa*-lath-*coom*
Fos	foss
Fusci	*fuh*-skee
Gven'bahr-brum	g-*ven*-bah-*brūm*
Kemal	kem-*al*
Koos	kooss
Leulah	*loo*-luh

Ludder's End	*luh*-der's *end*
Mahrulan	*mah*-roo-lan
Mylanfyndra	mill-n-*fin*-druh
Pyra	*pī*-ruh
Qendo	*ken*-do
Ryke'ven-apoth	*rīk*-ven-*a*-poth
Toova'ven-tuil	*too*-vuh-ven-*twee*
Umfalen	um-*fah*-lun
Valen	*vah*-len
Wurthen	*wer*-then (hard th)

COMMON WORDS

athlynder-skyrr	ath-*lin*-duh-*skeer* (the final accent is lighter than the first)
charnon	*chah*-nun
durrerry	duh-*re*-ri
fremma	*frem*-uh
hetzan	*het*-zun
issalm	*iss*-alm (l is sounded)
koury	*koo*-ri
leoia	lee-*oy*-uh
medron	*med*-run
podlith	*pod*-lith
podlithra	pod-*lith*-ruh
skyrring	*skeer*-ing
thruyl	thray (soft th)
wyrth	weirth (as in weird)